## "Vivienne! Look out!"

She heard a roar behind her, saw Caleb draw his gun and start to move. Pivoting, she froze for a split second. A speeding car was bearing down on her. Hank!

Her arms waved, giving the dog direction as she dropped the end of the leash. "Go! Go!"

Spinning on his haunches, the border collie did exactly as ordered. He took off running—away from her.

Had she not taken that precaution, she would have had more time to guard her own body. By the time she looked back to see where the speeding car was, it was nearly upon her.

### *TRUE BLUE K-9 UNIT: BROOKLYN*

*These police officers fight for justice with the help of their brave canine partners.*

**Valerie Hansen** was thirty when she awoke to the presence of the Lord in her life and turned to Jesus. She now lives in a renovated farmhouse on the breathtakingly beautiful Ozark Plateau of Arkansas and is privileged to share her personal faith by telling the stories of her heart for Love Inspired. Life doesn't get much better than that!

### Books by Valerie Hansen

#### Love Inspired Suspense

#### *True Blue K-9 Unit: Brooklyn*

*Tracking a Kidnapper*

#### *True Blue K-9 Unit*

*Trail of Danger*

#### *Emergency Responders*

*Fatal Threat*
*Marked for Revenge*

#### *Military K-9 Unit*

*Bound by Duty*
*Military K-9 Unit Christmas*
*"Christmas Escape"*

#### *Classified K-9 Unit*

*Special Agent*

Visit the Author Profile page at Harlequin.com for more titles.

# TRACKING A KIDNAPPER

## VALERIE HANSEN

**LOVE INSPIRED** SUSPENSE

INSPIRATIONAL ROMANCE

Special thanks and acknowledgment are given
to Valerie Hansen for her contribution
to the True Blue K-9 Unit: Brooklyn miniseries.

LOVE INSPIRED® SUSPENSE
INSPIRATIONAL ROMANCE

ISBN-13: 978-1-335-72185-3

Recycling programs
for this product may
not exist in your area.

Tracking a Kidnapper

Love Inspired
22 Adelaide St. West, 40th Floor
Toronto, Ontario M5H 4E3, Canada
www.Harlequin.com

Printed in U.S.A.

I may as well swing by your place on the way. If you won't do it for yourself, do it for your partner."

Rising, she stretched. "Well, since you put it that way."

"I do."

"Oh, and Caleb," the sarge said, "if you'd like to offer your assistance on Vivienne's case, too, we'd appreciate it. I'm sure as an FBI agent, you've dealt with plenty of kidnappings."

Vivienne froze. Did her boss just actually assign the guy to work with her?

"Happy to help," Caleb said, eyeing her.

Vivienne intended to follow the two men, but they took up positions on either side of her as they left the promenade. She didn't object. Something intangible and indescribable kept sending little bolts of electricity zinging up her spine and tingling the nape of her neck. She might have discounted those feelings if her K-9 hadn't been acting as if he, too, was disturbed.

"Your dog," Gavin said. "See how he's acting?"

"Yes. I've been watching him."

Caleb slowed his pace and pivoted, his back to the others. "I'm not used to working with K-9s but this one is sure antsy. I take it that's not normal."

"No," Vivienne said. "Border collies can be high-strung, but Hank should be pretty tired. Instead of relaxing he's on alert. See his posture? Tail position? The way he's moving his ears? He's picked up on something the rest of us haven't."

"You two wait here to minimize exposure," Gavin said. "I'll get my car and be back in a sec."

If the humans had been the only ones acting tense Vivienne might have argued. Since Hank was so restless she opted to take her sergeant's advice. Someone was either watching them or trailing them—someone who had Hank on alert. Vivienne glanced around but didn't see anyone suspicious.

Caleb looked around, too. "I don't see anybody, but that doesn't mean we're not being followed or watched." He sidled closer to her, placing his body as a shield. Vivienne knew what he was doing and took the action as a sign he didn't think she was a fully capable officer of the law.

"I am not helpless, you know," she said.

"Never said you were."

"Well, you're acting like it so back off. A bullet could just as easily pass through you and take me out." The instant she spoke he whirled around, staring at her. His color seemed paler,

his green gaze more intense, and she could see the muscles in his square jaw clenching. If she'd been the profiler instead of him, she might guess he'd once been in that very situation.

"I'm not moving," he said, "so deal with it."

Recalling what he'd looked like without his jacket, she was positive he wasn't wearing a protective vest. Unfortunately, neither were she and Hank. It was the dog that concerned her the most. The stubborn man could look out for himself.

"Suit yourself," Vivienne told him in a pseudo sweet voice. "I'm going into that recessed doorway over there to protect my K-9 whether you like it or not."

"Why didn't you say so?"

She traded a chuckle for a huffing sound at the last second. Nobody liked to be laughed at, and agents who were the strong, silent type were the worst. Plus, this one was a man. Male egos bruised easily. They were going to have to work together, at least in theory, so the happier she could keep him, the better.

Not that she was going to bend over backward to please him. She simply didn't want to purposely make an enemy. Besides, unless her imagination was working overtime there had been something poignant, almost tender, about

his expression when he'd first approached her. Of course, she'd been cuddling Jake and Hank when he'd arrived with her boss, so maybe he merely had a soft spot for kids or dogs, or both.

"Hank, heel," she commanded, pivoting in the narrow recess of the doorway and positioning herself to look out with the dog seated on her left side. It didn't surprise her when the FBI man reassumed his position in front of her like a sentinel.

"I do appreciate your concern," she said, hoping to make peace.

"But?"

"But this really is a peaceful, upscale neighborhood. You must know that the original houses bordering the promenade have been restored and sell at a premium if they're ever put on the market."

"Rich people are no different at heart than the disadvantaged," Caleb argued. "The same thing goes for criminals. Push someone too far and anything is possible."

He had a valid point. She smiled when he glanced back at her. "I grew up right here in Brooklyn."

"Family?"

"A much older brother who moved to the West Coast. My parents are gone." *Which is another reason why I crave a family of my*

*own*, she added silently. There was still time left on her biological clock, but that didn't mean she was willing to let those years slip away. "What about you? Do you have extended family close by?"

All he said was "No," but the undertone convinced her there was a lot more to his story than simply being a widower.

Vivienne squelched a strong urge to pat him on the arm. To offer comfort for his sadness. She knew better than to touch him and chance having her gesture of compassion misunderstood.

Caleb leaned forward to peer up the crowded street. "I think I see your boss's car coming."

"Good." Suddenly, he extended his arm and abruptly pushed her back. If he'd explained she wouldn't have had to ask the question. "What's wrong?"

"Across the street. You can't see her face right now because her phone is in front of it. I think somebody is taking your—our—picture."

Vivienne peered past him. "Where?"

"Right below that Open sign in the drugstore window. There. She's lowering her phone. Look."

"No hoodie, but..." Vivienne inhaled a gasp.

"I think that *is* the kidnapper. How did you pick her out?"

"Instinct. Her intensity. And the fact that taking a lot of photos is typical of a fixation."

"But why now? Why me?"

"A guess? She's ticked off that you stopped her and wants to remember you and your K-9."

"Terrific. If I try to go after her, she'll run. Do you think you can get over there and grab her without being noticed?"

"I can try."

Vivienne figured it would have been an easier task if Caleb hadn't been so tall and well-built. There were enough businessmen on the street to keep his clothing from being different, but his height was a definite disadvantage.

He cupped a hand around his mouth, evidently meaning to speak to her privately. Vivienne leaned closer to hear. As he bent slightly she heard the singing crack of a gunshot. It echoed back and forth between the taller buildings, making it impossible to accurately pinpoint origin or direction of travel. Actions of passersby, however, told a clearer story.

Caleb instinctively ducked. So did she. Some people on the sidewalk screamed and dodged while others across the street, where the shot had apparently come from, ran for their lives,

pushing each other aside and falling down in a wild effort to escape.

"Get down!" Caleb shouted, stepping out despite the danger and waving his arms. "Everybody down."

That was enough to spur more action with the majority taking cover.

"Inside," Vivienne yelled to him as she leaned hard against the glass of an exterior door leading to upstairs offices.

She and her K-9 partner made room for Caleb. When he joined them seconds later, he was swiping at his short, darkish blond hair and what looked like fine rubble was falling to the floor.

"The kidnapper took a shot at me?" she asked. "Why?" He brushed at the gray powder on his suit jacket.

Without thinking, Vivienne began to help him dust the back of his shoulders. "It could have been random."

Frowning, Caleb said, "You can't be serious. We just spotted a probable criminal right across the street. She was looking straight at us and taking pictures. She must have been armed, too."

Vivienne sighed. "With all the police hanging around down here you'd expect any shooter to be more cautious."

"If he or she was sane to start with," Caleb replied, scowling as he went on to report the incident by cell phone and request backup.

The face in the hoodie flashed into Vivienne's mind. Those eyes. That flushed skin. The way the woman had been clutching the child. Now that she thought about it, no part of the woman's demeanor had struck Vivienne as even marginally normal.

Her sense of accomplishment over recovering the boy faded. She was now a kidnapper's target, likely for foiling the woman's crime.

She peered past Caleb. Gavin's patrol car was nosed into the curb less than twenty feet away. Half a dozen police officers were taking defensive positions while others held back curious onlookers. Everything was typical. Except—

Vivienne grabbed Caleb's forearm and pointed. "Look! Unbelievable. I think she's still over there!" It was hard to swallow past the dry-cotton feeling clogging her throat.

Gavin had left his car idling and he joined them. When Vivienne tried to point out the woman she and Caleb thought they had identified in the crowd, she had vanished.

# THREE

Rather than pick up his black SUV and head back across the bridge to FBI headquarters in Manhattan, Caleb followed the Brooklyn group back to their station. He told himself he was merely there to make sure Vivienne didn't leave out any details in her report, but even he didn't fully buy that excuse. Nor was he willing to dive deep enough to analyze himself. He'd had his fill of his own and experts' questions about the tragic assault that had cost him both his wife and their baby son. Yes, it hurt. It still did and probably always would. But he'd learned to live with those memories. To function despite personal pain.

The secret was to compartmentalize the past, Caleb assured himself. The same went for the present and what was to come. There was nothing to be gained by letting himself brood or relive events that couldn't be altered. That part of his life was over. It had ended in the

few agonizing seconds when his family had been obliterated. And with them, he realized sadly, had gone his joy, his faith and his hopes for the future. Settling into his job and focusing only on work had saved him, in a way, by keeping his mind from imagining what might have been and not making too many forays into his wounded psyche. It wasn't an ideal response, but it worked for him.

Entering the three-story limestone-faced building that housed the Brooklyn K-9 Unit, he smirked briefly. It took a pretty savvy agent to convince examiners that he'd healed when in reality the wound was still raw. Still painful. He'd known what they'd wanted to hear from him and had delivered pat answers on demand. He desperately needed to keep working, to feel useful. Necessary. Being sidelined might have literally killed his spirit.

The K-9 unit offices were surprisingly modern inside. Desks were arranged geometrically, and spare kennels had been stacked neatly against one wall.

Caleb hung back until Gavin addressed him. "Since you're assisting, I'd appreciate if you'd come into my office and listen to this debriefing, too, Agent Black. You may have noticed something the rest of us missed."

"Okay. Thanks." The dubious expression

Vivienne displayed was not nearly as welcoming as that of her boss. Nevertheless, Caleb followed.

Vivienne took the chair the sergeant indicated. Hank circled twice and curled up at her feet. Caleb could tell she was nervous. Who wouldn't be? Being shot at would do that to a person, even one as seasoned as he was. For all he knew, this might be the first time this K-9 officer had been under fire.

"The second look I got at the kidnapper when we were waiting for you to pick us up may help even more than my first encounter," Vivienne volunteered. "Don't you think I should meet with a sketch artist ASAP?"

Gavin nodded soberly. "I do. I just want to make sure I understand everything about the shooting. We can't be one-hundred-percent certain that it's connected to the attempted abduction, but it's probable."

Vivienne nodded.

Her smile was a little tremulous although she did seem to be recovering well, Caleb concluded. This was one resilient woman. That part of her character reminded him of his late wife. Too bad that being a cop hadn't saved her.

"As I said, the woman I saw was tall, wiry and thin, middle-aged," Vivienne said. "When

I saw her wearing the gray hoodie I couldn't tell what her hair color was, but in the crowd across the street from where Agent Black and I were standing, it looked sandy gray. Short and curly. A tight perm, although now that I think about it, she could have been wearing a wig."

Gavin looked to Caleb. "Do you think she was your shooter?"

"I do. The bullet impacted the stone above our heads and thankfully didn't ricochet into us. It could have come from an upper window across the street, but judging by the way the crowd scattered I assume they heard or saw a gun go off right next to them. That would be hard to miss."

"All right." Gavin turned back to Vivienne. "Write up a full report. I want every tiny detail, not just bare bones. I'll read over what the patrol officers got out of the boy's mother on the promenade and we can compare notes later."

"Yes, sir." She stood.

"I don't want you out on assignment for any reason without clearing it personally with me," Gavin said.

"Yes, sir."

"Caleb, perhaps you and Vivienne could compare notes, too, see if there's anything either of you saw or heard but didn't think to

mention." He turned to the K-9 officer. "Vivienne, I'll assign a patrol unit to drive you home when you're ready to leave for the day."

"I could take her and the dog," Caleb said, letting his feelings override common sense. Playing bodyguard was not in his job description.

Sergeant Sutherland's eyes narrowed as he studied them. "We'll see. Right now I want you to both wait in the outer office while I organize my thoughts. You go do the same."

That order didn't surprise Caleb, but Vivienne seemed unsettled. She made a face. "What was that all about? Sarge seems very comfortable with you. Are you two buddies or something?" she asked, wending her way between the desks and leading him into the break room.

Caleb shrugged. "Nope. But this is his domain so he's in charge."

Vivienne looked over the room with appreciation and sighed. "This old station and the building next door were recently remodeled to house our new unit. I love the beaux arts architecture, don't you? It was built in 1910. You don't see stonework like this on modern construction." After giving Hank a down-stay order, she crossed to the coffeepot. "Want a cup?"

"I don't know. Was it made this year?" Caleb deadpanned.

She eyed the glass pot. "Good chance. Maybe even this week."

"In that case I'll take a cup." He pulled out a chair from beside a small dinette table and sat.

"Cream? Sugar?"

"Black, thanks. With a name like mine I almost have to drink it plain."

To his relief he got her to smile. "Caleb Black. Right. So, Agent Black, what brought you into the FBI?"

"A search for justice and truth.'"

"Sounds heroic. Do you mean it?"

"Very much so. An unsolved murder in my hometown when I was a kid got me interested in law enforcement. I became a cop, then applied to the FBI and became a rookie all over again. Profiling came next. It was a natural fit."

"I've wanted to be a cop since I was a kid, too—just was always in awe of the uniform," Vivienne said. "I haven't been at it as long as you have."

"I'm not *that* old." He arched an eyebrow.

"I think it's the suit," she countered, smiling. "It makes you look so serious."

He took a sip of tepid coffee and tried to keep from grimacing. "I am serious. It goes with the job."

"Really? The people I work with do their

best to lighten the mood around the station. Keeps us sane."

Caleb laughed as he watched her realize what she'd just intimated about him. "Hey, I'm the profiler here, remember?"

"Sorry. I didn't mean it personally."

"Sure you did. It's okay. No offense taken. None of us is completely normal the way we assume civilians are. If we were, we couldn't bear the tragedies we deal with on a daily basis."

"Think so?" She joined him at the table while Hank rested beneath it on the cool vinyl. "I don't know if I buy that."

"Careful. You could be profiled."

"It might be fun," Vivienne said thoughtfully. "I've often wondered what made specific people behave the way they do. I don't mean hardened criminals. I don't need to know if their parents were mean to them or they failed English class in school and that ruined their lives. What puzzles me is why one sibling turns to crime while another leads an upright life."

"Well, when you figure that out please let us all know." He paused, sipped, made a face and set aside his mug. "Take the woman you were chasing this morning, for instance. She may be part of a gang that steals children or

somebody who craves a child and can't have one. Or she may want a little boy for some obscure reason that's not yet evident. Whatever her trigger is, she's apparently the kind who holds a grudge." Pausing in his analysis, he saw Vivienne shiver.

"I don't see why else she would shoot at me."

He nodded. "Her, or an accomplice we didn't notice when we spotted the kidnapper taking photos of you."

As they compared notes on all the details, as Sgt. Sutherland had asked, Vivienne wondered aloud if the shooter would try again.

After leaving Hank to nap in one of the kennel runs in the K-9 training center next door, Vivienne reported to the interview room. Instead of pencil and paper, the bejeweled, brightly clad woman waiting for her had brought a laptop and was seated at the table.

Vivienne offered her hand. "Hello. Vivienne Armstrong. Sorry if I looked surprised when I came in. I'd expected Eden Chang."

"I'm Danielle Abbott. Eden's busy and I was free so they sent me over from the Command Unit." Danielle bestowed a joyful grin as she shook hands, her bracelets jingling. "Don't worry about doing this. Just trust me and your memory."

Mirroring the smile, Vivienne joined the tech-savvy forensic artist at the table, where she was opening her laptop. "You don't actually draw the face, right?"

"In a manner of speaking, I do. We use a computer program that creates the features. You and I will go through this program together, step by step, and you can decide when we're done."

"I'm not sure I remember enough."

"That's a typical fear. Don't sweat it."

"Okay, I…" She startled when someone knocked on the door.

Danielle called out for the person to come in, and Caleb entered.

"Caleb!" Danielle greeted him with a wide grin. "Good to see you again. It's been ages since I did a reconstruction picture for you."

He nodded. "Sorry to interrupt—I know you're about to start. I just wanted to let you know I'll be waiting outside to see the finished product. I wish I could be of more help, but I only got a look at the woman from a distance."

Vivienne knew he'd come for moral support. She gave him a smile and nod, then turned to Danielle. "Okay, I'm ready."

He smiled back with a you've-got-this expression and left.

Vivienne couldn't help being curious. "You know him well?"

"Well enough," the tech guru said with a sad smile. "He's had it pretty rough."

"He told me he was widowed."

Distinctly penciled eyebrows arched. "He did? He actually said it? Out loud?"

"Yes. Why?"

"Because he usually keeps everything about his past to himself. At least he used to. If he's talking about it these days, that's a very good sign."

Vivienne was slowly shaking her head. "I don't know. He acted awfully grumpy and only said one word. *Widowed.*"

"That's understandable, given how he lost his wife and baby to a killer who was after him, instead." She shook her head.

Vivienne inwardly gasped. She'd had no idea.

"Nevertheless," Danielle continued, "he mentioned it. Do you have any idea what triggered him to reveal that?"

"I think it was because I noticed him fiddling with his wedding ring. He still wears it."

"Yeah, I know. Sad, isn't it?"

"Not to me," Vivienne said. "I think it makes clear that he loves his late wife even though

she's gone. Someday I'd like to find a guy who will love me forever and ever."

Danielle smiled. "They're definitely out there. I found one."

"When and if I ever find the right man and fall in love, I'm committing for the rest of my life…and beyond. Somewhere out there is the perfect husband, someone who was meant for only me."

"Then I hope you find him the same as I did," Danielle said, reaffirming with a new smile. "In the meantime, what do you say you and I get busy? We'll put together a likeness of the kidnapper that we can circulate to all patrol officers."

"Right. Since she didn't get away with the Potter boy she may focus on another child soon."

Although the woman nodded in agreement, Vivienne knew what else she was thinking. Then Danielle added, "Or take another shot at you and your dog."

"Yeah, there is that possibility. I hope it doesn't keep me from working in the field." She remembered feeling sorry for K-9 unit detective Henry Roarke and his beagle partner, Cody, when they were sidelined for a few months. Not to mention Noelle Orton and her yellow Lab partner, Liberty, who were cur-

rently having their duties curtailed because of a bounty being put on the K-9's head after a successful arms raid. "I'd hate to be stuck doing desk work all day."

"Better for you to stay off the streets than to be carted off in a body bag."

Vivienne scowled. "You do have a way with words."

"Just tellin' it like it is, or can be. I've been to too many cops' funerals in my career. None of them can count on going home at night and don't you forget it. So please be vigilant."

What Vivienne wanted to say was that she trusted God to look out for her. Unfortunately, she also realized that her faith wasn't meant to be used like a talisman. If she truly trusted Christ she also had to be ready to accept His will for her life. Even if she didn't live long enough to fall in love with the perfect man and raise the family of her dreams? she mused. She shivered again, battling nameless fear, and the answer was *yes*.

# FOUR

Caleb stalled as long as he could before re-joining Vivienne and Danielle. He'd wanted to ask to stay, to see if he could help, but he'd been afraid his influence might hamper the efforts at identification, and he also wanted to get a look at the finished product, not just bits and pieces as the women put it together. Seeing the face morph into its final shapes could adversely affect a person's memory, distorting it until mistakes were made despite efforts to recall details accurately.

When he knocked on the door to the interview room and stuck his head in, he was prepared to back off. Vivienne's broad grin showed him it wasn't going to be necessary.

He smiled back at her. "Done?"

"Yes. At least I hope so." Vivienne pushed back her chair. "Come tell me what you think."

"What *you* think is what matters. You saw

her up close. I just caught a glimpse across a busy street."

She nodded, got to her feet and urged him closer to the laptop displaying the face. "True. But I was anxious and you were calm. That has to make a difference."

"It can," Caleb said kindly. "Sometimes being on edge will wipe out a person's memory completely. Other times, nerves can imprint on a mind so thoroughly that the image lingers for years. Maybe longer. Studies have shown uneven results."

Danielle nodded. "That's because it's practically impossible to scare somebody out of their wits when they know it's an experiment."

"Very true." He sidled past Vivienne and made his way to the table, where he could peer over Danielle's shoulder. The "drawing" was black and white, and looked as if it had been hand-drawn with a pencil or maybe charcoal. The kidnapper's skin looked wrinkled and droopy on a thin face and the eyes were narrowed, as if squinting. Her mouth turned down at the corners, completing a very unpleasant countenance.

"There is something familiar about her," Caleb said. "I only got a glimpse, mind you, but you've captured her menacing aura."

"I thought so, too," Vivienne said. "I sug-

gested we picture her with short hair instead of wearing that gray hoodie because she didn't have it on when we saw her on the street."

"Good idea."

"Glad to hear it's a solid composite," Danielle said.

"Have we heard from any of the investigating officers on scene?" Vivienne asked. "Were they able to come up with witnesses who saw her shoot at us?"

"No." Caleb sobered and shook his head. "You know how it can be. Unless a family member or friend is the target, bystanders often plead ignorance."

"They may do that even if it's not a loved one. I've never understood making that choice. I mean, you'd think they'd stand in line to give evidence that would put the bad guys in jail."

"It depends on the situation," Caleb said. "Sometimes the criminals have stronger influence than family."

"Is that what happened in your case?"she asked gently.

Caught by surprise, he didn't know how to respond. First of all, he wasn't aware that she knew about his past. Second, he'd been asked plenty of questions before, but never one phrased quite like Vivienne's.

"In a way, yes," he finally said.

"No wonder you go about your job the way you do. I'm really sorry."

Caleb watched empathy fill her expression. She seemed to intuitively understand his deep-seated need to catch and punish the man who had ruined his life, stolen his joy and his future, yet it was hard for him to accept sympathy.

"The assailant was identified and arrested," Caleb said flatly.

"Sentenced?"

Latent anger began to rise as Caleb remembered the charges leveled at the trial. Attempted murder for trying to kill Caleb. Manslaughter for the deaths of his wife and baby. His jaw clenched. He struggled to keep control of his temper.

Vivienne seemed to see into his heart. "No punishment can be equal to what you've suffered. Even if their killer had received the death penalty in a state where it's still legal, that wouldn't have been enough to take away the pain. Not even close."

Touched, yet determined to keep from showing it, Caleb stood very still, back ramrod-straight, chin lifted in defiance. If she kept talking about his loss, he wasn't sure how he'd respond. As a fellow law-enforcement officer, she was merely trying to be kind and offer

moral support, he knew, but he had almost reached the limits of his tolerance. Men and women he worked with daily were well aware of his reluctance to discuss the worst day of his life, so they didn't prod. But Vivienne Armstrong had no knowledge of his unwillingness to talk.

The forensic tech had been quiet during the conversation, but clearly heard something in his voice that told her he'd had enough. "So what do you say we get this show on the road? I'll email this file to all precincts and see that we get printouts, as well."

Danielle was smiling with her mouth, but Caleb could tell by her eyes that it was forced. He whipped out his cell phone. "Send it to me, and I'll see that my unit is informed, too."

He gave her the number and waited until he'd received the drawing, then offered his hand with a simple "Thanks."

"Anytime." She laughed softly. "I'm like a kid. Sometimes it's hard to make myself go back to work after a field trip."

"How about lunch?" Vivienne asked her. "I know a place that permits K-9 partners if you don't mind pizza."

"Mind? Girlfriend, I was raised on the stuff and if you mean Sal's, you can definitely count me in." She paused and looked at Caleb. "How

about you, FBI? Loosen your tie and you'll fit right in."

"I've been to Sal's. They don't have a dress code."

Chuckling, Vivienne said, "They will for my Hank. I'll go get him and his working harness, change into my spare uniform and meet you in the front office. We can walk over."

Caleb nodded. Danielle held up a hand to offer Vivienne a high five. "Gotcha. Can't wait."

As soon as Vivienne left, Caleb turned to Danielle. "Thanks."

"Nothing to it. You looked like you were getting ready to explode. All I did was change the subject."

He inhaled noisily. "Yeah. It's been seven years, but I still have trouble, particularly if I think I'm going to have to explain the details again. It's not like I forget. I'll never do that. But talking about the details can hurt like taking a bullet myself."

"I get it." He ran his index finger inside the front of his shirt collar and partway around his neck, then loosened his tie. "I'll open up more about it to Vivienne if it becomes necessary for some reason. I don't expect to be here long. I'm only on loan."

"Checked out like a popular library book?"

Danielle laughed. "When are you going to get back into circulation, anyway? You can't brood forever."

He wanted to say "Yes, I can," but decided to treat her comment as the light-hearted observation she'd intended. "Too many dog-eared pages and a tattered cover on this book," he said with a slight smile. "There's a lot of mending yet to do." Opening the door, he held it for her.

"It's what's inside that counts," she insisted. "And don't you ever forget it."

The crowd at Sal's was thick, as usual, with a line out the door and down the sidewalk for those waiting to buy a slice to go. Those who chose to get a whole pizza or pasta order had filled all but one table in the rear and Caleb led the way to it with Danielle, Vivienne and Hank close behind.

Having the working dog along helped clear a path. So did Vivienne's blue uniform. He did, however, wish she'd also kept an extra belt and service weapon at the K-9 unit so that she'd be armed if need be between here and home. The station was certainly a more secure location to leave a duty weapon than any apartment in the city.

Caleb turned to her. "Dog on the outside?"

"Yes, please. He'll scoot under the table but it's easier for me if he has access to the open area." She gestured. "After you."

Danielle chose the right side of the table and loaded the fourth chair with her laptop and voluminous purse before sitting down. Caleb had little choice but to make room and welcome Vivienne on his side. It was crowded, to say the least.

"I should have ordered for us before we sat down," he said, starting to push back his chair.

"Not a problem. This was my idea, so I'll take care of it." Vivienne smiled at him and Danielle. "Instead of telling me what you like, how about keeping it simple? Just tell me what you hate."

"I'm good with the basics," Caleb said. "It smells so good in here I may die of hunger before we're served."

"I know." She chuckled. "How about the Sal's special and a pitcher of ice water? Or would you rather have soda?"

"Water's fine," Danielle said.

Caleb nodded in agreement. "Me, too."

He reached for his wallet, but Vivienne waved it away. "This is on me. If you want dessert after we polish off an extra large special you can buy it. Personally, I doubt any of us will be hungry when we're done."

He watched her place Hank on a stay with the flat of her hand in front of his nose, then she jostled her way through the crowd. Caleb sighed. Unfortunately, Danielle noticed.

"Ah-ha. You like her, don't you?"

"I like everybody. You know that."

"Do not. I know for a fact that you're put off by that blonde receptionist at your Manhattan office."

He rolled his eyes. "'Put off' is right when it comes to her. I've never given that woman one reason to think I was interested in her and she won't give up."

Danielle's grin widened, her eyes sparkling. "That's because you're irresistible."

"Oh, please."

"I'm serious. It's your wounded heart that gets 'em every time. They want to hug you and make it all better. It's an instinctive female thing."

"So how do I put a stop to it?"

"Move on, I guess." She made room on the table as Vivienne returned carrying an icy cold pitcher and three glasses.

"They'll call *Armstrong* when the pie comes out of the oven. In the meantime, drink up. It's hot outside."

"What about Hank?" Caleb asked.

"He has his own dish and I gave him plenty

to drink back at the station. We discourage our working dogs from eating or drinking anything that isn't offered properly and by the right person. Hank has me."

"Suppose something happened to you?" Caleb asked. "What would he do then? Starve?"

"Nothing is going to happen to me." Her smile waned. "At least I hope not."

"I've had my eye on you the whole time we've been out," he assured her.

Danielle giggled behind her hand. "That's the truth."

He blushed. "Don't pay any attention to her. She has a weird sense of humor."

"Don't we all?" Sliding in next to him, Vivienne bumped his shoulder and Caleb imagined the temperature in the already warm little restaurant had risen twenty degrees.

He busied himself pouring ice water into all the glasses and sliding them across the slick tabletop to his companions. More than one businessman in Sal's had already stared at their party as if he wished Caleb would share—and he didn't mean the water. Being in the company of two good-looking women would normally have been quite enjoyable. This time, however, it was making him decidedly uncomfortable. Danielle was laughing at everything

and Vivienne was smiling, too, although she was also blushing. Therefore, his attitude had to be the problem.

As a profiler he didn't have to wonder what was wrong with him. He knew he turned moody whenever he was even slightly attracted to a woman and in this instance he found himself unable to keep from admiring Vivienne Armstrong. She was more than attractive—she was witty and smart and braver than many he'd met in law enforcement. Under normal circumstances that might be all. In this situation, however, he considered himself her guardian and protector. It didn't matter whether that was part of his official assignment or not. It simply was.

Again, he couldn't help making a comparison to his late wife. He'd been lax in his defense of Maggie and she had been taken from him. Was he being given a second chance? As far-fetched as that sounded, Caleb wondered if it might be true, at least in part.

So what if it was? That only meant he needed to be extra vigilant, not that Vivienne was destined to take Maggie's place. No one would ever do that. No one could measure up.

Plus, Vivienne was a cop, too, just like Maggie had been. A confident officer of the law whose job was to put herself out there and protect the citizens of Brooklyn and all of New

York City. She may as well have had a bull's-eye painted on her uniform.

Caleb's stomach churned and not from hunger. The more he thought about it, the more he realized he was beginning to care too much. Any degree of personal interest was too much as far as he was concerned. So how in the world was he going to stop his feelings when his job and her job had brought them together and might keep them in close contact?

Answer: he wasn't. Sergeant Sutherland had specifically asked him to work with Vivienne on the kidnapping case. Meeting her that first time on the promenade had led to this moment and probably many to come so he may as well get used to it. Accept it. Deal with it as best he could, then put it all behind him as soon as he was free to leave Brooklyn.

Given that he was working with the K-9 unit to find Randall Gage, whose DNA had been found at the crime scene of the McGregor double homicide twenty years ago, *and* that he was helping Vivienne track down the kidnapper, he wasn't leaving Brooklyn anytime soon. And granted, his headquarters was just across the river in Manhattan, but given the population of the city his chances of accidentally running into Vivienne afterward were slim.

That notion settled in his heart and gave him

pause. They barely knew each other, yet he was already certain he was going to miss her.

"Armstrong" blared from the PA system and bounced off the walls.

Caleb pushed away from the table as soon as Vivienne stood and sidled past her with a brusque "I'll get it."

What a relief it was when she let him go. He blinked back the unwelcome moisture gathering in his eyes and lost himself in the crowd on the way to the counter. By the time he was ready to return, he was certain he'd have regained his self-control. That was crucial, both to his stalwart image as an agent and to his carefully crafted, unruffled persona.

It had been a long time since he'd grown this emotional in public. He supposed thinking about losses of all kinds had gotten to him. Hopefully, it would be a longer time before it caught him by surprise and happened again. If he hoped to convince others that he was fine, he was going to have to do a much better job of proving it to himself.

And that began here and now. He scanned the crowd as he passed through. A flash of movement near the exit caught his eye, then was gone. Caleb stared. Anything abnormal could signal a threat. He couldn't afford to overlook the slightest clue.

On high alert, he headed for the door. Peered out. Saw a shadowy figure in a gray hoodie disappearing in the distance. Coincidence? He didn't think so.

Turning, Caleb headed for the pickup area at the counter only to see Vivienne carrying their meal to the table herself.

He caught up with her. "Hey. I said I'd get that."

"For a minute, it looked like you decided to leave." She stared up at him. "What were you doing?"

There was no choice but to tell her, regardless. "I spotted something suspicious, so I went to check it out."

"And?" Vivienne had paused at the table, still holding the tray with the pizza on it.

"And I saw somebody running away. He or she was wearing a gray hoodie."

Caleb caught the tray as Vivienne's hands began to tremble, settled it on the table and pushed her into the farthest seat so he'd be between her and the door.

"You—you didn't give chase?"

"Too far away. We could call the station right now and report the possible sighting."

Vivienne shook her head. "Forget it. It may not have been the kidnapper. And any identifiable threat is already long gone, as you said, plus we can check the security-camera footage."

"True." Caleb gestured at their steaming lunch. "We may as well dig in."

Danielle reached for a slice and dragged it onto her plate. "I love a sensible man," she quipped, "especially when I'm starving and he offers food."

Pretending to be amused, Caleb served Vivienne and himself, then began to eat. His concentration never wavered from the doorway for more than a few seconds. If the person he'd seen returned, he would be ready.

# FIVE

Vivienne barely tasted her meal. Oh, she ate, of course, but the pizza might as well have been made of cardboard. While the company sharing her table kept her fascinated, like Caleb, she was constantly checking the people in the crowd.

Danielle kept up a lively banter. Caleb gave one-word answers or comments as they ate. Having conversed with him before in full sentences, Vivienne was concerned that she may have offended him by asking about his lost family. What she should have done was wait until she could speak to Danielle in private again and get more personal details from her. She knew the basics but perhaps it would help to know more.

*Why do I need details at all?* she asked herself. *Good question.* One with no pat answer.

"So," Danielle said as she blotted her lips and started to gather up her gear. "This has

been fun but it's time for me to boogie. I have plenty of work waiting for me back at my regular post. Glad to be of help when you guys were in a bind, though."

Caleb stood. Vivienne got to her feet, too. "Okay. I guess it is getting late. We don't want to hog this table with so many hungry New Yorkers waiting for a place to eat."

"You two go first," Vivienne said. "I'll bring up the rear with Hank." She could tell by the stern look Caleb gave her that he didn't like her choice of being unprotected from any angle. Thankfully, he didn't argue…this time.

Out of habit she reached to hitch up her utility belt and check the position of her sidearm, then realized with chagrin that both were waiting at home. Hank heeled. As their party of three and a K-9 reached the exit she morphed into cop mode as easily as always and that gave her added confidence.

Caleb was holding the door open. Danielle passed through first, tossed off a quick wave and headed for the subway.

Vivienne looked around for the gray hoodie but didn't spot it. Caleb seemed to be surveilling the area, too. They'd just reached the center of the wide sidewalk when the dog froze in his tracks.

Frowning, Caleb was at her side. "Why did you stop?"

"I didn't. Hank did." She was scanning their surroundings again, as was the FBI agent. "I don't see any threats, but this dog is never wrong."

"Never?"

"The only thing that might throw him off is a flock of sheep coming down the middle of the street." Although she was tense, she managed a smile. "See any?"

"Nope. Your precinct is close by. Let's get going." He reached for her arm.

Vivienne evaded him. "Do you seriously think I'm going to let you shepherd me around like one of Hank's imaginary lambs?"

"Sorry. Guess I'm too used to being in charge."

"You're forgiven." There was a time for asserting independence and a time for listening to wise advice. This was the latter, particularly since she was unarmed.

She rolled her eyes and headed back toward the station at a brisk walk. Hank reluctantly paced beside her, looking back from time to time until they were actually inside the building again.

"Conference room," she said flatly, gesturing to Caleb. He wasn't smiling. Neither was

she. As soon as they were alone in the separate room she pulled out her cell and dialed.

"Who are you calling?" Caleb asked.

"Eden Chang. She's our usual tech guru but she had the morning off. She's likely in the station now." Vivienne held up her hand, signaling Caleb to wait. "Eden? Vivienne Armstrong. I need you to check any video cameras that show the streets near Sal's in the last half hour or so. That's right. The pizza place. And while you're at it, scan the ones covering our station, too. You're looking for a thin, middle-aged woman with a tattoo on her ankle. She may be wearing a gray hoodie. Okay? Thanks."

She ended the call and turned to Caleb. "Satisfied?"

"For the moment. Hank must have caught the scent of the kidnapper just before. Could anything else have set off your dog? And don't tell me he smelled a lamb's wool coat. It's August."

That comment brought a smile. "I can't get over how observant you are, Agent Black. You noticed right away that nobody was wearing a heavy coat."

"Or a hoodie, since we're comparing intellects," he countered.

She started for the door. "I do think she

was hanging around nearby Sal's, waiting to catch me alone, perhaps." She glanced down at Hank. "I'm going to kennel Hank while I go home to get my gun. When I get back, I'll start whittling down the pile of paperwork that's accumulated since this morning."

He shrugged and followed. "Seems like a lot longer than that, doesn't it?"

"Oh, yeah. I think I've aged ten years."

"You look like a teenager when you're out of uniform. How old are you, anyway?"

"Old enough to have a degree in law enforcement and have completed specialized training as a K-9 handler. I'm twenty-eight. Come on. Let's put my K-9 to bed."

They left the station by a side door and were passing through a grassy open space between the K-9 unit and the training center next door. Police cars were parked in designated spaces on Bay Ridge Avenue, blocking her view of the street.

Suddenly, Hank dropped to the ground, flat on his stomach. Milliseconds later Vivienne heard a shot and feared he'd been hurt. She hit her knees, hunched over her K-9 partner and reached for her gun…that wasn't there.

Caleb covered for her. He took a shooter's stance over the pair lying on the grass, ready to fire.

"Do you see anybody?" Vivienne shouted.

"No." He sidestepped and passed her. "Stay down."

"As if you have to tell me!" A cursory examination was all it took her to realize Hank had reacted as trained and dropped at the threat of shooting. He was not only unharmed, but was also wagging his tail, as if proud of himself.

She, however, was breathless and her heart was pounding. Caleb had his back to her. He'd reached the front sidewalk and was scanning left and right, still ready to fire. That was fine as long as one of the other officers stationed there didn't take him for an assassin and drop him where he stood.

The leap to her feet was wobbly but quick. She held out her arms to block several men in uniform who had raced out the side door brandishing firearms at the sound of gunfire. "Stand down!" she yelled. "He's FBI. Shooter in the street."

Caleb must have heard her, too, because he raised both arms, his pistol pointing skyward, and started back toward her while her colleagues fanned out.

"Is the dog hit?"

"No." Embarrassed to be so emotional about it, she sniffled and fought tears of relief. "He's better trained than I am."

"He had a faster response time than either of us," Caleb said as he holstered his gun. Then he started shaking hands with the nearby officers and simply said, "Thanks."

"Did you see the shooter?" Vivienne asked him.

"No, unfortunately. But hopefully your colleagues will find her." Vivienne assumed a wide stance, fighting to balance without showing how unsteady she felt. "I'll go kennel him now."

At her feet, Hank circled and pranced, clearly eager to be taken to his kennel, where he could drink and rest.

Those antics were just what Vivienne needed. Smiling at the happy dog, she reached the door to the training building and punched in the access code, a little surprised when Caleb didn't rush ahead to open the door for her. Clearly he knew she'd be safe in the training center. And maybe she liked his chivalry more than she'd been willing to admit. As long as he respected her as a police officer, he could open all the doors he wanted for her when they were operating as civilians. That made sense.

*Sense? Hah!* The words echoed in her thoughts, making her focus on the irony of the situation. The only thing that actually made any sense lately was her rescue of the little

Potter boy. Anything after that included Caleb Black and struck her as total guesswork.

They were guessing why the kidnapper was trying to kill Vivienne. As payback? They were guessing why the boy had been snatched in the first place. Plus...

Vivienne continued her line of thinking as she kenneled Hank and gave him fresh water. Plus, she finally added, she was guessing at why she seemed so drawn to an FBI agent she barely knew and why his personal losses had hit her so near the heart.

After talking to the K-9 unit officers who'd looked for the shooter—no sightings—Caleb had trailed Vivienne and Hank into the kennel area and waited while she'd tended to her valuable dog. Once again, although he'd been on his guard, someone had gotten off a shot without being detected. If the assailant had been a better marksman the outcome could have been tragic.

She patted Hank, told him goodbye and latched the gate behind her.

"How can you smile after what just happened?" Caleb asked her.

"Because of my dog. And these others," Vivienne said, sweeping her arm in a wide

arc while a dozen nearby canines of various ages sounded off. "This is my happy place."

"How do you stand the noise?"

"They're just doing their jobs. You're a stranger, and we disturbed their afternoon naps."

He raked his fingers through his short hair and shook his head. "I could use one of those after the morning we had."

"Hey, I was the one who ran almost the length of the promenade."

"And we've been dodging bullets ever since. I forgot to ask. Did your sergeant say if they found any shell casings?"

"They didn't. If this was the same shooter a few minutes ago and he or she used the same gun, they probably won't this time, either."

"Right. So we can assume they have a revolver."

"Either that or somebody else picked up their ejected brass, which is pretty unlikely," Vivienne said. "I'm sure our guys are going over the street very carefully."

"Mmm-hmm." Caleb set his jaw. His assignment was to profile a murder suspect and perhaps tie him to a more recent homicide that had the same MO, not shadow a K-9 officer as if he was her stalker.

Following Vivienne back to the K-9 unit,

they stopped to talk to the sergeant and gave a report, then he trailed Vivienne to her desk. She sat down and swiveled her chair to face a computer keyboard.

"I thought you were going home to get your duty gun."

"I was. I am. Sarge doesn't want me to go on my own and none of the officers can drive me right now." She stared at him. "Don't you have something else to do?"

"Yes. And no. Are you trying to get rid of me?"

"I might be." She blushed. "I'm not used to being shadowed all the time. It's a little unsettling."

"So is taking a bullet because there's nobody there to watch your six."

With a telling sigh, she stood. "Tell you what. I'll go change back into my street clothes, sneak out the back door and take a cab home."

"No, Vivienne. It's not safe. Wait for me— *inside.* I'll check in with your sergeant and let him know I'll take you home and back."

The off-putting expression on Vivienne's face failed to make him feel reassured, but he proceeded, anyway, positive she would be sensible enough to follow his instructions. It wasn't that he considered the streets of Brooklyn particularly dangerous—it was simply the

apparent bull's-eye on this particular officer that gave him pause. For some crazy reason—other than the obvious—he was beginning to feel responsible for her welfare.

Going straight to Sutherland's office, Caleb found it empty. He stopped at the first cubicle to ask where their boss had gone, then worked his way across the room with no success.

"All right, plan B," Caleb muttered. Unsure of the layout of the main floor, he left by the front door and circled the building to get his SUV and pick up Vivienne. Judging by prior experience waiting for his wife to dress to go out, he figured he still had plenty of time for Vivienne to change back into her street clothes.

Caleb's jaw clenched. *Maggie again*. Always Maggie. Whenever he showed interest in another woman his late wife made an appearance in his thoughts. He didn't mind. At least he hadn't until recently. Right now, this second, it was Vivienne Armstrong he need to focus on.

Pulling around the corner of the building, he drove past a dented green trash receptacle and scanned the perimeter. The station exit was clearly marked and was keypad protected, so he couldn't easily go inside. Therefore, he'd wait. Surely it wouldn't be long before the K-9 cop emerged.

His heart reopened to thoughts of his late

wife. A casual glance around was instinctual…
until he saw a familiar jogging outfit and a
young, athletic woman climbing into a taxi in
the distance. "Vivienne!"

She never faltered, didn't look back. Caleb
was astonished, then angry. He grabbed the
steering wheel and sped after the departing
cab. If she thought she could ditch him, she
was in for a surprise.

Seconds later an older model, tan sedan
slipped into traffic directly behind the cab.
Caleb whipped around it as soon as he had
an opening. He was not going to lose sight of
her no matter how erratically the cabbie drove.

# SIX

Vivienne smiled as she climbed the interior stairs to her third-floor apartment. It seemed a bit strange to not have Hank at her side, but not worrying about him right now was a relief. She wasn't proud of ditching her tall, handsome shadow, but she wasn't going to let Caleb Black boss her around. She'd told him she'd take a cab and she had.

She let herself in, shedding her jogging clothes on the way to the shower. She turned on the water, and by the time enough hot water had reached her apartment she had a fresh uniform laid out and her duty equipment waiting. That made redressing a snap. So did her short, easy-to-care-for haircut. A couple swipes of the brush and a touch of lipstick and she was good to go.

The belt was heavy with the holster, flashlight, cuffs, radio and extras for her K-9. She had it buckled and was reaching for the door-

knob to head back to work when someone hit the door so hard it shook.

Instant reflexes had her palm on the grip of her pistol. "Who is it?"

"Me!"

That was all the introduction she needed. Caleb Black had somehow followed her and was less than thrilled with her leaving him behind.

As soon as she checked the peephole, she opened the door. His fist was raised, ready to pound again.

"Hi."

"Hi? That's all you have to say?"

"Um…hi, Agent Black?"

He pushed past her. "Very funny. Not. What did you think you were doing taking off like that? By the time I got here and found a parking place you could have been dead."

Extending both arms in a display of well-being, she smiled at him. "As you can see, I'm fine."

Clearly, he was fighting with himself to regain more self-control. Although he wasn't shouting at her she could tell he was still plenty upset. Well, too bad. She was a cop, not some damsel in distress who needed coddling. Nevertheless, it was nice to see concern even if it was misplaced.

"You drove?" she asked.

"Followed your cab."

"Great. Then you can drive me back." She strode past him to the door, opened it and walked through. "Coming?"

To his credit he followed, jerking the door closed behind them and giving the knob a twist to make sure the apartment was secure.

"Where did you park?" Vivienne asked lightly.

Caleb gestured. "Next block."

Gruffness in his tone remained and she didn't know why she felt the urge to placate him. After all, she was a well-trained officer of the law and she was now fully armed, including her smaller ankle gun. She didn't need a plainclothes bodyguard and it was high time he accepted that fact.

A brief pause at the outer door was enough to show her there was no danger, no stalker waiting to harm her, so she pushed it open and bounced down the stone steps onto the sidewalk. "Left or right?"

Caleb pointed with his key ring, keeping it in hand to unlock the car doors. Once they reached the SUV she was able to climb in before he circled and slid in to drive. His hands gripped the steering wheel so tightly his knuckles whitened. Strong hands. Capable

hands. A good man. A good agent. And, in a way, she had let her sense of independence hurt him.

As soon as her seat belt was fastened Vivienne reached out to lightly touch the sleeve of his jacket. "I'm sorry. I shouldn't have ditched you. It wasn't nice."

"It wasn't safe," he snapped back.

"There were a lot of cops still out looking for the shooter. I knew I'd be okay so I called a taxi service to pick me up."

He sighed. "You should vary your habits. And the times you travel."

Vivienne wanted to make him feel needed so she agreed. "Under the circumstances, that may be a good idea until we catch the kidnapper, who's clearly trying to take me out."

"No. All the time."

"Really?"

"Yes. You need to be more wary, more cautious about everything you do."

"It's not good to act paranoid," she said, positive he would accept her conclusion.

Instead, Caleb glared over at her and said, "You're only paranoid if nobody is after you."

Once Vivienne had returned to her desk and got busy working, Caleb was able to relax. He was still mad at her but no longer furious, the

way he had been. The intensity of emotion had been a shock at the time. It was one thing to be upset or disappointed about a coworker and quite another to invest so much of himself that it tied his gut in knots and made him act unprofessionally.

Thankfully, she didn't seem to be holding a grudge.

"So do you plan to stay right there and finish your paperwork?" he asked.

Considering the way she rolled her eyes and arched her eyebrows, she hadn't totally forgiven him. "Unless I'm dispatched to another incident. Why?"

"I thought I'd go talk to Penelope McGregor and see if she can recall anything new that might help my deductions. I know she's been interviewed many times the past several months and that she was very young when her parents were murdered, but she may have ideas that she didn't voice before."

"It's better than trying to interview Lucy Emery," Vivienne said, leaning back. "Poor little thing was really scared after the murder of her parents. She's only three. If her aunt Willow hadn't taken her in immediately afterward, I don't know what would have become of her."

Caleb was relieved to be back to discussing business. "Murders of two sets of parents

twenty years apart and leaving a young daughter alive in both cases. Add the clown mask the killer wore and his gift to each child of a stuffed monkey toy, and you have enough similarities to suspect the same perpetrator."

"We only have a DNA match in the McGregor case," Vivienne reminded him. "What would make a guy like Randall Gage wait twenty years between crimes? I mean, if he's really a heartless murderer I'd think he'd keep at it, wouldn't you?"

"That's one of the things I have to decide when I profile any criminal," Caleb told her. "They may have similar patterns of behavior or be totally different in all but a few critical areas. That's why every little detail matters."

"Have you talked to Lucy's adoptive parents? Willow Emery, her aunt, and Nate Slater, one of our K-9 cops, got married and are providing a safe home for her. They live right here in Bay Ridge."

"I saw that in the file. I'll get to them. I want to start with Penelope McGregor. Sergeant Sutherland says she works here in the station. Reception, right? I'd planned to talk to her yesterday but never got a chance."

"Want me to introduce you?"

"That won't be necessary. I'll stop by Gavin's office on my way. If he still isn't there,

I'll wing it." Worry lines began to crease his forehead again. "You won't leave the building?"

To his relief Vivienne smiled. "Okay, okay. I promise I will sit right here until—" she glanced at the precise time posted on her computer screen "—until at least five. How's that? Will it suit you?"

"Well enough. Understand, I'm not trying to boss you around. I've been present during attempts on your life. That's not something to take lightly."

Nodding, Vivienne stopped laughing. "Yeah, I know. I'm just not fatalistic about it. I have faith that God has put me here for a purpose and He'll be with me until the job is done."

She paused, studying him so intently it made him uncomfortable. When she continued, she definitely touched a raw nerve. "Are you a believer? A Christian?"

Caleb took a deep but shaky breath. "I used to be," he said. "Not anymore."

Sitting very still as Caleb walked away, Vivienne felt bereft. Crisis always brought a change, sometimes for the good, sometimes not. A person had the chance to choose an upward path, trust God and try to make the most of his or her own life. Or they could opt to give

up. To reject spiritual help. To turn away from their faith, even to deny God. And then what? Then, they floundered just as Caleb Black was demonstrating.

Sadly, she had never felt right preaching to others. In Caleb's case there was no way she could reason away his sorrow or explain why good people died and evil ones lived on. The problem was not solvable that way, nor would it ever be. Some survivors nursed survivor's guilt for years while others grieved differently, thanking God for the blessings of the past and stepping forward into whatever life had in store for them.

"It's the difference between joy and happiness," she told herself quietly. "Happiness depends on circumstances. Joy is deeper and eternal."

A broad, cold nose poked her in the elbow as a friendly voice said, "That's right."

Vivienne jumped. "Oh, Belle! You startled me." She reached past the cold nose and scratched the huge German shepherd under his chin. "Good boy, Justice."

"Where's Hank?" the other K-9 officer asked.

Sighing and swiveling her chair to face Belle Montera and her protection-trained K-9, Vivienne gestured with a lift of her chin. "Next

door in the training center, resting. We had a tiring morning."

"So I heard. Where's your good-looking bodyguard? Gavin said an FBI agent was watching your back and working with you on the kidnapping."

"Who says he's good-looking?"

"Every woman I've asked," Belle responded with a grin. "And judging by the way you're blushing, you think so, too."

"He's one of those brooding guys that bring out our motherly instincts, I guess. That's why I was thinking about happiness versus joy. He doesn't seem to have either and it's painful to watch him suffering like that."

Belle huffed. "Really? What does he do, go around with a long face all the time?"

"Not exactly. Most of the time he seems fine. The thing is, he's not okay deep down inside. I've only gotten a glimpse of his pain." She leaned close to whisper. "He lost his wife and baby to a shooter who was reportedly out to kill him, and I can't even imagine how he feels."

Belle leaned away, aghast, causing Justice to tense up and visually search the office for a threat. "Whoa. How awful." She laid a calming hand on her dog's head. "It's okay, boy. Take it easy."

Vivienne understood how in tune the K-9s were to their partners, so she didn't fear the big shepherd. It was actually a relief to see him ready to defend Belle and anyone else she sent him to. "Yeah. The thing is, he seems to be stuck in the angry stage of grief instead of moving on to healing. He has a short fuse."

"What makes you think he'll ever change?"

Shaking her head slowly, Vivienne tucked her hair behind one ear and pressed her lips together, then said, "I pray he will. I know he'll never forget the terrible loss, but for his own sake he needs to come to terms with the fact that there is more to life than the past. Right now he's so wrapped up in the tragedy he doesn't realize that he can have a good, worthwhile future."

"How long has it been?"

"That's irrelevant," Vivienne answered. "No two people grieve the same way or at the same speed. As a profiler he surely knows that there is no chart, no perfect progression, for things like that."

"And that matters to you because…?"

Vivienne was reluctant to postulate. She shrugged. "Beats me. All I know is that he blames himself. That's who he needs to forgive."

"You plan to talk him into it?" Belle looked incredulous.

"No. No way. My job is to accept him as he is. Caleb believed in God once. He can embrace that again. And once he does, I truly believe his faith will bring him through."

"Sounds to me like he's mad at God, too."

"Probably. I imagine I would be if I'd placed all my trust in Him to protect my loved ones and they'd been killed. The thing is, we don't see the whole picture. It's like the murders of Penny and Bradley McGregor's parents twenty years ago. The aftermath brought Penny to work for us and Bradley became a great K-9 detective."

Belle began to smile. Her cheeks colored. "Carry that notion further and you can see that it also brought my Emmett to Brooklyn. We might not have met otherwise."

The other woman's obvious delight gave Vivienne a jolt of unearned jealousy. Belle Montera and US Marshal Emmett Gage had each other. Willow and Nate Slater were already married. Raymond Morrow and Karenna Pressley were madly in love. Even K-9 unit member Henry Roarke had found bliss with Internal Affairs officer Olivia Vance, yet here Vivienne sat, unattached, unmarried and running out of time to see her dreams of a family come true despite joining those dating apps as a last resort. It wasn't fair.

Then again, she reasoned, perhaps the recent attempts on her life indicated that her future was going to be short.

She struggled with that unwelcome concept. Granted, no Christian was promised a lack of trials, but they were assured that the Lord would be with them no matter what. It wasn't a matter of blindly accepting disaster. It was more the opportunity to do the right thing at the right time and then trust the Lord with the outcome.

Belle had to run, so Vivienne bid her colleague goodbye and turned back to the computer. *Trust* was the secret, the answer to temporal questions regarding infinity.

It was okay to not be omniscient, to not control the universe, to admit to being human and confused. Which was where Vivienne was at the moment. She didn't know why she cared so much about Caleb Black's faith and his future. She just did.

An internal shiver shot up her spine and made the roots of her hair tingle. Someone currently had her in his or her crosshairs and was trying to end her life. That was a fact.

And God had provided extra protection in the form of an FBI agent. For that she should be thankful. God would handle the rest. She just wished she had a hint about how.

# SEVEN

Caleb's time in Gavin Sutherland's office should have been short and uncomplicated. It was not.

"I hate to disagree with you, Sergeant," Caleb said, "but you need to find somebody else to work with Officer Armstrong from now on and to keep her safe. My superiors did not send me over here to babysit."

"No, they sent you to help us figure out if Randall Gage killed both the McGregor parents and the Emerys or if we're dealing with two killers. But since you were right there with Vivienne when the kidnapper shot at her, I thought you'd want to work with her on finding the woman."

He did. But… Things were getting complicated. "I want the kidnapper caught and the threat against Vivienne gone. But I also need to focus on the profile. I want to interview Penelope McGregor as well as Willow Emery.

I plan to do that separately, although I know they've been interviewed many times."

The sergeant nodded. "Detective Slater and Lucy's aunt, Willow, are caring for the girl and whenever Lucy comes up with some new remark pertaining to losing her parents we're immediately informed."

"I'll take the McGregor crime first. I've read the file and pulled up the old newspaper reports, but as I said yesterday, I'd still like to hear the story from Penelope herself."

"I'll buzz her and let her know to expect you. While you're talking to her I'll put in a call to your unit chief and get his okay to use your skills as I see fit."

Caleb didn't like the implication. Nevertheless, he kept his thoughts to himself. His position was as secure as he could make it, considering the mandatory time off he'd had to take after his family tragedy. Yes, he knew his superiors kept their eyes on him, just in case, but he'd passed all his evaluations and had been certified as emotionally stable. There was nothing anyone could do to prove otherwise.

*Unless I make a mistake,* he added, leaving the sergeant and weaving his way to the reception area, where the first person on his list waited.

A young, red-haired woman rose from behind the front desk, smiled and extended a hand. "You must be the FBI profiler."

Caleb shook her hand. "Yes, Caleb Black." He looked around the area. "Can you get somebody to sub for you so we can talk in private?"

"Sure." Still smiling slightly, the brown-eyed clerk circled her desk, spoke to a co-worker, then joined him. "All set. I'll take my afternoon break now."

"We can use one of the interview rooms. Would you like to grab a coffee first?"

"I'll get a bottle of water later. Follow me."

As he did so, Caleb noted her tall, slim grace. Pictures of her older brother, Bradley, showed the same basic coloring, although his hair was more of a dark auburn. It would be interesting to see if little Lucy Emery had any freckles or red in her hair. Every possible connection had to be compared.

Penelope led the way to an empty cubicle at the rear of the large squad room. "Will this do? I really don't like to sit in those tiny spaces where we question suspects."

Glancing around, Caleb nodded. "Okay. We'll keep our voices down so we don't disturb anybody."

She sat in an armless chair, leaving the desk open for him, and Caleb took his place at it.

He'd memorized enough of the files to know what to ask without referring to past answers. Part of his job was to put the subject at ease and explain what he would be trying to do.

Leaning forward, he assumed a relaxed pose. "The human mind is a funny thing, as you probably know. If it isn't sure about something it will often fill in the blanks with what it thinks fits. That's what happens when we see one of those scrambled sentences and are surprised to be able to read them. Our mind has sorted out the confusion."

Penelope was nodding, watching him intently, so he continued.

"That can also happen when someone witnesses a crime, which is how a dozen witnesses can come up with as many differing descriptions. They're all telling the truth as their brains have interpreted what they saw."

Sighing, she said, "So by this time, what I think I can recall about what happened twenty years ago has to be far from reality. Is that what you're saying?"

"Yes, and no. You were interviewed right away, and you were very young at the time. You wouldn't have had a lot of life experience to draw on. That helps, in a way."

"I still have nightmares about the clown

mask. Not as often as I did at first but they do still occur."

"Does it always look the same to you in your dreams?"

"It had white and red paint on the face and blue hair. That's about all I remember."

"Okay. What about the toy monkey the killer gave you before he left?" Caleb saw her try to hide a shiver. "Have you ever seen another one like it?"

"No, and I hope I never do." She folded her arms across her chest and hugged herself. "It should be stored in evidence if you need to look at it."

"It is. It's not exactly the same as the one left with Lucy Emery, of course. I wouldn't expect it to be identical this many years later."

He paused to give Penelope time to calm herself. The trauma had obviously left scars on her psyche regardless of whatever counseling she'd received as a child. "Right now I'd like your impressions. Never mind searching your memory for details. Just talk. Tell me whatever pops into your head."

"Anger. And fear. You'd think I'd be over it by now, wouldn't you? There are days, weeks even, when I honestly don't think back to those terrible events. When there was a killing on the twentieth anniversary of losing my parents

it all became fresh again, as if I were going through it with Lucy."

"I'll be speaking to the Emery girl soon. I wanted to start with you to keep the events chronological."

"How will that help Lucy?" Penelope asked. "We know Randall Gage's DNA matches the sample on a watchband found at my house all those years ago. I'm so thankful the police kept all the evidence safe in storage until it could be properly tested using newer forensic methods."

Caleb nodded. "Right." The team had gotten lucky with a hit from an ancestry site, leading to a relative of US Marshal Emmett Gage. As hard as it was for the marshal, he'd identified his cousin Randall Gage as the probable suspect, then had managed to get Randall's DNA to prove the match. But Randall had gotten away twice since and was still at large.

"But what about Lucy? Was he responsible for killing her parents, too? I mean, if he was, why wait so long between similar attacks?"

"That's one of the questions I hope to answer," Caleb said. "Close your eyes and let your mind drift back. We know what you remember seeing. How about hearing? Or smell? Was his voice familiar?"

"No. I don't think he said much of anything."

"How about strange odors? Odd or unpleasant?"

Penelope squeezed her eyes shut tight for several seconds. When she finally spoke, Caleb was disappointed to hear her response. "Sorry. Nothing."

"Okay. I hate to ask you to dwell on something so traumatic but I'd appreciate hearing about any little thing that pops into your head, even if you don't think it matters." Caleb handed her his business card for reference. "My cell is on here. Call anytime. Day or night."

"All right." She checked her watch. "I should be getting back to my desk."

He stood when she did and thanked her. Like it or not, asking victims to recall their traumas was often the only way to learn enough to put together a proper profile. Firsthand commentary plus police records formed a more complete picture. All he had to do was extrapolate on the facts without letting his imagination interfere.

His jaw clenched. Yeah, like when he involuntarily recalled the personal trauma that had cast a dense shadow over his life for the past seven years. It had morphed into a tolerable sense of loss, but it never went away. Never.

A sudden urge to check on Vivienne Arm-

strong stopped him in his tracks. This was the first time he had realized how connected he felt to her. Admitting it, even to himself, was decidedly unsettling.

Worried about her friend and coworker, Vivienne lingered in the reception area of the police station, waiting for Penny to return from being interviewed. One quick glance at the younger woman's face told her what a trial the session with Caleb had been.

Vivienne opened her arms and offered a consoling hug. Penny hugged her in return, then took her usual seat behind the counter, ostensibly looking over the waiting messages and other notes. Vivienne wasn't fooled by the diversion. "Bad time, huh?"

"I've had better."

"I'm sure you have. Which reminds me, have I told you about my latest blind date?" The lopsided smile she saw arising on her friend's face was exactly why she'd changed the subject and brought up the funny story.

"Another success?"

"Oh, yeah. Totally. I'm not sure whose picture he posted online but it sure wasn't his. Still, I figured it was only fair to give him a chance so I stuck with it. Until he excused himself to use the restroom and split."

"He stuck you with the bill?"

Vivienne chuckled. "Oh, yeah."

"What did you do?"

"Well, first I ate my dessert. Then I ate his. And then I paid the tab and waddled home." She rubbed her stomach dramatically. "Ate too much and learned another lesson."

"Which was?"

Vivienne was delighted to see the amusement in Penelope's expression, the sparkle in her eyes, so she embellished her answer.

"Well… I learned that people sometimes lie."

"Duh." The younger woman rolled her eyes. "You just figured that out?"

"Confirmed it," Vivienne said. "I've decided it's taking me too long to find Mr. Right. I may never realize my dreams of mothering a big, happy family."

Penelope was encouraging. "You have plenty of time. Your biological clock may be ticking, but you have time. Keep looking."

"And praying to be led to the perfect man," Vivienne added. "According to Danielle Abbott from the NYC K-9 command, they do exist."

"That's a relief," Penelope said. "Hey, what about considering my big brother, Bradley? He's single."

"He is sweet. And good-looking. Unfortunately there's no chemistry between us."

"Maybe you're going at this wrong. Maybe you should be thinking with your brain instead of your heart."

"Uh-uh. I don't want to get married only for the sake of making a family. I intend to marry for love and let the rest come as God blesses. I wouldn't even care if the guy had a few kids already. The more, the merrier."

"If you say so." She shuffled the stack of memos on her desk. "Maybe you've already met him and just haven't recognized the attraction yet."

Vivienne sobered. "I kind of hope not."

"Why?"

The truth stuck in her throat and she briefly considered keeping it to herself. "Well, it's this way. I'm not sure that what I've been feeling lately is for the right reasons and it's left me in limbo."

When Penny glanced back the way she'd come, Vivienne followed her lead and noticed Caleb Black standing across the room, watching. Was her interest that obvious? she wondered, hoping otherwise. Admittedly there was something about the FBI agent that drew her, yet those sensitivities might be skewed by pity, among other things. There was a certain pull to a man who was permanently out of reach the way Caleb Black was. Any woman who

fell for an emotionally wounded guy like him was bound to be hurt in the long run.

Part of her—the sensible part—agreed. The part of her that understood loneliness and commiserated with him kept asking if it might not be worth taking a chance.

Internally laughing at herself, Vivienne shook her head. Why speculate about an opportunity that would never present itself? Wishful thinking couldn't take the place of prayer for discernment and trusting the Lord to lead her to the perfect partner. Her job—her only job—was to stay out of God's way and not try to run His universe for Him. Surprisingly, that was hard to do.

"Right now, my biggest problem is staying alive long enough to fall in love with the man of my dreams," she told her friend. "I'd better go pick up Hank and do some refresher training before I think too much and get depressed. See you later."

With a final quick glance in Caleb's direction, she turned and fled the station, expecting him to follow. The intensity of the stare he'd been leveling at her stuck with her all the way out the door and beyond.

She was crossing the grassy alley to the building next door when she heard a loud bang, like a gunshot, and realized with dismay that

she'd been so lost in thoughts of Caleb she hadn't bothered to check the alley for threats.

Vivienne hit the ground, rolled and drew her gun. She bounced up into a shooter's stance, staying low, and swung her aim in a protective arc. Perspiration dotted her forehead and made her hands slippery. Her pulse pounded in her temples, her breathing rapid and ragged.

She'd almost let daydreaming bring her down. Worse, it had been errant thoughts of a certain man that had nearly cost her the very life Caleb had vowed to preserve.

Three men burst from the station's side door, Caleb in the lead.

"Where did the shot come from?" he demanded.

"I don't even know if it was a shot," Vivienne told him. "If there was a shooter, they fled when you three came out."

Other officers joined them and fanned out to cover the alley.

Turning away from him, she shouted to her fellow officers, "Anybody see anything?"

Negative replies did little to settle her nerves. Neither did the uncomfortable closeness and aura of power coming from the FBI agent beside her.

# EIGHT

Caleb had been reading lips and trying to eavesdrop while Vivienne had talked to Penelope. It was his task to learn as much as he could about Penelope, so paying close attention hadn't bothered his conscience one bit...until he'd discerned bits and pieces of what Vivienne was talking about. He'd inched closer, unable to quell his interest.

The conversation about finding a mate had torn at his heart in a way he hadn't expected. Could she have been referring to him? Both women had looked his way so it was certainly possible. That would never do. He had to make Vivienne understand that he was not in the market for another wife, let alone a family. Love hurt too much when it ended. And the deeper it was felt, the worse the pain.

And yet... Caleb's brow furrowed. His sense of great loss lingered, yes, but it had become slightly hazy, as if softened and perhaps not

quite as clearly defined. That realization did not sit well with him. He didn't want to forget, to adjust, to give up the strong connection with his missing loved ones that he'd been holding on to for so long.

Before he could muse further his cell phone rang. "Black." The caller was his immediate superior, not the unit chief, but that hardly mattered considering the message.

"We're making one of our safe houses available to you and the K-9 cop you've been assisting," the agent said. "I'll text you the address. Continue with your previous assignment but move her and the dog into the safe house with you for the time being."

"But—"

"No buts about it, Agent Black. The commander of the K-9 unit has requested it and we've gotten it cleared with the higher-ups."

Caleb pulled the phone away from his ear and stared at it. If he'd been a suspicious man, he might suspect that Vivienne's boss was playing matchmaker, which was way out of line. There was only one way to find out. He went straight to the sergeant's office, knocked once, then walked in.

Sutherland looked up. "What's wrong?"

Caleb shut the door. "I hear you made an

official request that I look after one of your people."

"I told you I was going to ask for that option."

"I don't think it's in Officer Armstrong's best interests for us to spend extra time together. You need to choose somebody else."

"I disagree." Gavin picked up a piece of paper from his desk and held it out. "Take a look at this screen capture from outside the station. See the orange tattoo on the ankle?"

"Looks like a flower."

"Tech thinks it's a lotus, whatever that is. But that's not the kicker. Here."

Caleb hesitated.

The sergeant thrust another piece of paper at him. "Take it. It's a record of a phone call Dispatch received for Officer Armstrong. It won't bite."

*It might,* Caleb thought, slowly reaching for the note. He blinked. Cleared his throat. Re-read the cryptic words aloud. "'You can't get away and neither can your mutt.' When did you get this?"

"Date and time are recorded. It was hand-delivered to me a few minutes ago."

"Vivienne never said anything about it. Does she know?"

"Not yet. I've asked her to come see me. She should be here any minute."

Caleb was about to hand everything back to Gavin when the subject of their conversation arrived, knocked and eased open the door. Seeing him there, she seemed reluctant to enter.

"I'm sorry. I didn't mean to interrupt," she said.

"Come in," Gavin said, motioning to her. "And close the door. This concerns you both."

As Caleb stepped back to give her room and she joined the small group, Gavin gestured to him. "Let her see the picture and that threatening phone memo before we get to the other details."

Caleb watched as she read the transcript of the telephone call for the first time, then he said, "Now look at the photo."

"Umm. Not good." She passed the papers back to him and he handed them off to Gavin. The sergeant gestured at nearby chairs. "Have a seat. Please. I was just discussing something with Agent Black."

Vivienne sat but fidgeted. "It's been almost half an hour since this phone threat came in." Her words sounded like an accusation. "Why wasn't I informed immediately?"

The expression on her boss's face showed disapproval. "I'll let that go because you're

under duress, Vivienne," Gavin said. "Bear in mind that whatever is done here is for your own good."

Because Caleb had been watching her, their gazes met and locked when she turned to him with a frown. "What's going on?"

Gavin explained. "You'll be staying in an FBI safe house here in Brooklyn for a few days. And don't look at Agent Black that way. It wasn't his idea, it was mine." He harrumphed. "He's no happier about it than you seem to be."

"Terrific. What about my K-9? Hank can't live just anywhere. He has needs. Requirements. Does this house have a fenced yard? If I have to walk him on the street it will negate any benefits of supposedly being kept hidden."

Caleb broke in. "I'll make sure there's everything Hank needs. It shouldn't be for long. If I can put up with it, you can." *Uh-oh. Bad choice of words*, he realized, seeing a flash of hurt in her demeanor.

She recovered rapidly, squared her shoulders and sat straighter in the armless chair. "Fine. I will have to go back to my apartment again to pack a bag. I can get K-9 equipment and dog food here, but I'll need clean uniforms and a couple other changes of clothes."

Looking to Gavin, Caleb wasn't sure he was

going to permit the side trip, so he offered, "I'll go with her if you want."

Sergeant Sutherland nodded. "Okay. Go. Vivienne, I'll want you to report by phone as soon as you're settled in the FBI house."

"Yes, Sarge," she replied. "After I go off duty."

"No. Go now. Before I change my mind and ship you off to New Jersey." Gavin shooed them out with one hand as he picked up the receiver of his phone with the other.

Caleb held the door for Vivienne, then followed her out. "Where to first?"

"My apartment. I have two roommates, but neither is home right now. One is a flight attendant and the other is on a trip to visit family."

"That's handy. Then you won't have to worry about them."

Vivienne gasped. "I hadn't thought of that. They'll need to be warned, too." She was slowly shaking her head. "What a mess."

"No worse than most cops face," Caleb reminded her. "You're just more identifiable because of your K-9 partner."

"I'm not leaving him behind, if that's what you're hinting at."

He held up both hands in mock surrender. "I wouldn't dream of suggesting such a thing."

"See that you don't," she replied, making a

face. "Where I go, Hank goes. I told you. He's not supposed to even accept food from anybody else."

"I imagine that can get bothersome if you want to do anything personal for longer than a few hours."

"Hank is totally worth it," she countered.

"I don't doubt that." Caleb was trying to be more agreeable. He didn't blame her for the intense reaction to the safe house. His own had been less than stellar. Nevertheless, they were both law-enforcement officers and had responsibilities to their superiors and comrades in arms. In Vivienne's case, that also included her K-9. She and Hank were looked upon as a single unit—a functional human with superior senses provided by an intelligent dog.

Vivienne turned misty eyes to him and asked, "Truth?"

"Absolutely. What do you want to know?"

"Your opinion. Nobody can be sure if that phone threat is legitimate. I want to know what your training and instinct is telling you. Should I be worried about Hank?"

"Always," Caleb said quietly. He stepped closer to her and spoke softly to keep their conversation as private as possible. "Even if that particular threat isn't serious, I think your dog should be protected at all costs." He cleared

his throat. "Except in a case where it's either him or you. I don't want to see either of you harmed."

"But you disagree on my using the safe house?"

"No, no." Shaking his head and moving both hands in an erasing motion, he met her steady gaze with one of his own. "I think it's a fine alternative for you. I just don't see why our bosses are insisting that I stay there, too."

"At least we agree on one thing," she said sharply. "Come on. I'll get Hank and his gear so we don't have to come back here after we pick up a few things from my apartment. While you're driving, I'll text both my roommates to make sure they don't come home unexpectedly and put themselves in danger."

He nodded and seemed lost in thought for a moment.

Leading the way through the grassy alley once more, Vivienne said, "Why can't criminals understand we're just doing our jobs? It's nothing personal."

"Now there's where you and I don't agree," Caleb said. "For me, it's very, very personal, particularly when I'm able to help an innocent child."

"Like Lucy Emery, you mean?"

Speaking past a lump in his throat, Caleb simply said, "Yes."

# NINE

Vivienne's mind was working a mile a minute as she prepped Hank for their time away from home and perhaps from the station, as well. It had occurred to her that Caleb's warning was right on. Anybody who'd managed to follow her and Hank from Bay Ridge when her shift ended could figure out where she lived pretty easily.

Seated beside Caleb in his unmarked black SUV, she watched the sidewalk and sized up pedestrians they passed. To her dismay she discovered that she was so keyed up she'd begun imagining an enemy lurking in every group. Although she kept trying to hide her physical reactions to those pseudo sightings, she wasn't surprised when Caleb asked, "Why are you so jumpy?"

"Um…" Vivienne quirked a nervous smile. "Bullets whizzing past my head? They tend to put me on edge."

"Oh, really? You could have fooled me. I thought you were worried about being stuck with me."

"What gave you that silly idea? I'm not a bit scared of you." *At least not in the way you're probably thinking*, she added to herself.

"Good to know." He leaned to look out. "We're getting close to your building."

"Yes. You can let me off and circle around while I grab my go bag if you want."

To her chagrin, he was shaking his head. "I'll find a spot. Don't panic."

"I *never* panic," she snapped, surprised when her remark came out sounding antagonistic. "Sorry. I guess I am more uptight than I thought."

"Understandable."

His calm demeanor and even tone needled her something awful. Staying in control was the goal of all law-enforcement officers, of course. It was just that in her case the attacks had become personal and thus she couldn't help taking them as such.

Memory of Caleb's previous reactions brought her thoughts full circle. Every now and then, his guard lowered just enough for her to get a glimpse of the man beneath the unruffled exterior. That was the real Caleb Black. That was the man who appealed to her—the

tenderhearted agent who could identify with frantic parents and minister to them with genuine empathy. That was the man she wanted to know better—the person who scared her... in a good way.

To get him to open up to her she was probably going to have to do the same and that was the frightening part. She would have to be so real that her heart would be vulnerable. And she was going to have to ask him to drop his guard, as well. *Could he handle doing that?* she wondered.

A better question was, could *she*?

"Is this spot close enough?" he asked, jolting her out of her poignant musings.

Vivienne leaned to peer out. "Yes. Grab it before somebody else squeezes past us."

"Not to worry. I drive in Manhattan, remember."

She had to smile at his parking expertise. "Smooth. If you ever lose your FBI job, you'll make a great cabbie."

"Good to know."

She was already unbuckling her seat belt and opening the door.

Hank joined her on the sidewalk, his tail high and waving with delight. "Sorry, boy, we're not staying," Vivienne told him. She

led the way to the outer door and punched in a code to enter the lobby.

Caleb stayed with her. "Stairs or elevator?"

"Stairs. It's good exercise."

She started to climb. "It seems as though we packed a week's worth of trouble into one long day."

"One very, very long day," he agreed. "I think tomorrow, unless you have a specific assignment, we should plan to interview the Potter boy and his mother. I know local patrols are keeping an eye on them, but I think we should suggest they leave town for a while, too." He and Vivienne had wanted to interview both Potters right after the kidnapping, but word had come back that both mother and son needed time to decompress.

"Sounds logical."

"Thanks."

She chuckled. "How do you know that was a compliment?"

"If it wasn't it should have been."

"That's one of the things I like about you, Agent Black—your humility."

As they reached the third-floor landing, Hank faltered. Vivienne immediately picked up on this change of attitude and stopped in her tracks.

Caleb followed suit. "What's wrong?"

"Not sure. Look at my K-9. He's gone into a crouch as if he senses a wolf about to attack his personal flock. That's us, by the way."

"Okay. Now what?"

"We take it slow," Vivienne said in a near whisper.

"What's that on the floor by your door?"

Vivienne took a step forward and peered down the dimly lit hallway. "I'm not sure. Maybe one of my roommates ordered something online."

"You didn't?"

"Not me. Anything I'd ever want is available right here in Brooklyn."

"Okay." He held out his hand to block her. "Stay right there. I'll go take a better look."

"No way." She gave him her most stubborn stare.

Caleb shrugged without giving ground. "Suit yourself. I thought you and that dog were supposed to protect each other. Is he a bomb sniffer?"

"No, he's a tracker. Still…"

"That's what I thought." He held up his cell phone. "Compromise. I'll call it in and you can give the other cops orders—or try to—when they get here."

Trembling as the possible contents of the unexpected package registered fully, Vivienne

eyed it with suspicion. If Caleb hadn't been with her and if Hank hadn't acted odd, she might have walked right up to the small, brown cardboard box and been blown to bits. Or not.

"It's not a bomb," she insisted. "It can't be. My enemies can't possibly know where I live."

"Suppose they followed your cab home earlier when you ditched me? Or maybe they followed me when I was chasing after you. Are you ready to stake your life on it? I can hold your dog while you go check the box."

"Oh, that's big of you. Thanks a heap. Protect the K-9 and let me go risk my life."

He huffed and grinned. "Hey, you're the one who insisted it was harmless. So go prove your point."

"I'll wait," Vivienne conceded, trying to keep from smiling and failing. "You win. This time."

Joking around helped her cope. Having the probably harmless package investigated and finding out she had been worried for nothing was going to help a lot more.

Surely that was what the outcome would be. Anything else was unthinkable.

Caleb noticed both K-9 and handler relaxing as the minutes ticked past while they waited for backup. He, on the other hand, stayed on

high alert. Vivienne's apparent nonchalance bothered him enough to mention. "I'd feel better about all this if you looked a little more scared."

"Really? You want me terrified?"

"That's not what I meant. You just don't seem bothered much by another attempt to harm you."

She rolled her eyes. "A *possible* attempt, you mean. We don't know that there's anything suspicious about the box. And even if the kidnapper-shooter did follow me earlier, the list of tenants only has the leaseholder's name— one of my roommates. Knowing that it's best for cops to keep a low profile we did that on purpose. So the perp wouldn't know which apartment is mine."

"Hank alerted."

She frowned. "True."

"I'd be more impressed with your precautions if you hadn't gone running off solo."

"Tell me you wouldn't have been tempted to do the same thing if you were in my shoes."

"There's no comparison," he argued.

"Why? Because you're a big, strong man and I'm a woman?"

Caleb huffed. "I'm surprised you didn't say 'just a woman.' That's what you were thinking, isn't it?"

"Maybe."

Did he dare tell her what had been going through his mind and why? A bigger question was, would it help? He didn't want to appear vulnerable in her eyes, yet it might be worth taking the chance if his confession resulted in the preservation of life.

Nodding, he squared his shoulders and faced her. "You'd be right if that's what you thought, but it doesn't have anything to do with you personally."

"I beg to differ. I'm the one standing here."

"But you're not the person who died because she was so sure she was equal to any man alive. My late wife was like that. She came close to winning, but she was also a mother and that's what ended up causing her to make the choices she did. Fatal choices."

Thankful that his voice was remaining strong and his emotions were staying in check, Caleb went on. "She thought she could out-smart an assassin who had come after me. And she was wrong. He turned the tables on her."

"I'm so sorry. You don't have to say any more if you don't want to."

"I think you need to hear it. You and Maggie are far too much alike. Oh, you don't look like her, but the same spark of independence and intelligence is in there." He pointed to

her head, intending only to make a point, and wound up tucking back a lock of her hair before he could stop himself.

Vivienne looked shocked but accepted the gesture without protest. He withdrew and stuffed both hands into his pockets, then gazed up at the ceiling, seeing the past instead of dingy acoustic tile.

"We knew a hitman was coming. My wife argued that staying with me was best because that way the killer would figure I was unaware and make his move while a task force was in place to capture him."

"That sounds logical."

"I thought so, too, at the time. I thought I could protect her, and she intended to protect me."

If Caleb had seen pity in Vivienne's expression he might have stopped his story right there. Because she was listening, wide-eyed and still, he kept talking.

"My wife decided, all on her own, to make a realistic dummy of me and stand it behind a shade so it threw a shadow. It was actually a brilliant idea. When she got it fixed the way she wanted, she went to get our son from his crib to feed him. On the way to the kitchen she insisted I go look at the dummy. She wanted my approval, that's all."

He paused to clear his throat, to try to squelch his emotional reaction to the telling of his story. "I was just coming into the room when I heard the first shot. A bullet hit the dummy and the force knocked it over." Despite tears welling he went on. "Maggie had our baby in her arms and I guess the natural reaction was to turn and shield him with her own body instead of hitting the floor the way we're trained."

Astonishment on Vivienne's face and shared pain in her eyes told him she already understood where his story was going.

"Yes," Caleb said. "The assassin had time to fire again. That rifle bullet went through Maggie's back and killed our son, as well. She died instantly. The baby died in my arms. He was so little, so innocent." He coughed to cover a sob and give himself a moment to recover. "Now do you understand why I lost my faith?"

She was nodding. "Yes, and no."

"It's not open to debate," Caleb said flatly. "God, if there is a God, failed me. Failed my family. I'm not telling you this to get sympathy or a lecture in theology. I'm telling you so you will understand why I need to make up for my mistakes. To protect other people and their children."

"I'm a cop, Caleb. I can protect myself and others, too."

"I know. I saw you save a child. What you and your K-9 do is vitally important and should be protected at all costs. That has become my job and I intend to do it to the best of my ability."

"So you feel you were lax in the past?"

"No."

The sparkle in Vivienne's eyes may have begun as unshed tears but it now resembled sparks of fire. Caleb tried to read her thoughts and failed. When she spoke it was with calm assurance. "Then stop blaming yourself. Evil exists. We see it every day. Some things defy explanation but that doesn't mean God has abandoned us. It simply means we don't understand. Yet. Maybe we never will."

"There's nothing left to understand. They're gone. Period."

"But you're here, Caleb."

"That's pretty obvious."

"And you feel a strong influence urging you to protect others, particularly children?" she asked.

"Yes. So?"

The way she slowly nodded, the way her gaze bathed him in peace, left Caleb wondering if she'd spout stale platitudes. He'd heard

enough of them over the years to fill a book and none had helped one iota. He braced himself, ready to fend off sappy feelings and stand strong regardless of what she said. It was bad enough that he'd almost lost it while telling her his story. He was not about to weaken further.

To his astonishment, Vivienne didn't tell him how sorry she was, although he could tell she commiserated. Instead, she gave him a sweet smile. All she said was "Good."

"Good? Of all the..." Caleb never got the chance to finish what he'd started to say because the small package on the floor in front of her apartment door began to smoke.

# TEN

Vivienne screamed. Ducked. Gave Caleb a push and dragged Hank after her. The ensuing explosion wasn't big, but it was plenty loud in the enclosed space. She covered her head with her arms as tiny pieces of ceiling plaster rained down on the stairwell. Hank hid behind her legs and Caleb grabbed her in a tight embrace, using his broad shoulders to absorb some of the onslaught.

Boots thundered up the stairs as helmeted officers carrying shields passed them. "Bomb squad is right behind us," one of them yelled. "Evacuate!"

Her ears hurt. The walls seemed to continue vibrating although she knew the puny explosion couldn't be having that much of an effect on the structure. In the grand scope of things, the little bomb had been ineffective. It had, however, proved that someone did know where

she lived and was out to terrorize her, whether they caused her harm or not.

That realization hit her hard. She began to tremble.

Caleb tightened an arm around her shoulders. "Come on. We don't need to be breathing this dust. Let's wait in the street and let the pros work."

She complied without thought, glad he was with her, doubly glad he was guiding her. She'd never admit it but having his physical and moral support was not only wonderful, but it also seemed very necessary. Her head was swimming and her eyes were itching and burning, blurring her vision.

Beside her, Caleb coughed repeatedly. So did Hank, although she knew the air was better closer to the floor. At least at the moment.

Once they were clear of the building, she crouched beside an idling fire truck, pulled Hank closer to check him over, then looked up at Caleb. "See if you can get bottles of water from somebody. Please?"

"Not leaving you. Whoever planted that amateurish explosive device probably meant it to at least make you run, if not do actual bodily harm. They could be waiting out here in ambush."

Chagrined, she had to agree. "Okay. You're

right. I guess it rattled me more than I'd thought."

That admission seemed to please him. Not that it should have mattered to her. After all, she was as much law enforcement as Caleb was, although in a different capacity. And yet, for some reason, she cared what he thought— what he thought of *her*.

The arrival of an ambulance completed the traffic jam. Nobody was going anywhere any-time soon. Vivienne was still shaking, and that bothered Hank as much as it bothered her. The intelligent K-9 knew she was scared. Really scared. Events had escalated so rapidly, as-suming they were all tied to her rescue of the Potter boy, that she'd been shoved off-center, off-balance. Add a handsome, caring, emo-tionally wounded kindred spirit to that mix and there were all the necessary elements for a meltdown.

Caleb was standing over her and Hank, keeping himself between them and the gath-ering crowd. Most of the spectators were be-hind police lines, but a few had managed to get closer and it looked as if everybody was intent on photographing her and her K-9. Cow-ering certainly didn't show her unit or the po-lice force in the best light. That wasn't how she

normally behaved, and no criminal was going to make her disgrace the badge.

Getting to her feet and dusting off her blue uniform, Vivienne tapped Caleb on the shoulder. "I'm taking Hank with me to the ambulance. You coming?"

"You're staying right here."

She arched an eyebrow. Tilted her head slightly. The shadow of a smile insisted on twitching at the corners of her mouth. "Don't think so."

Pivoting, he grasped her shoulders and stared into her watering eyes. "What do they have to do to make you a believer, Armstrong, level the block?"

"I'm already a believer, only not the way you mean," she snapped back. "My faith isn't built on everything going my way, it's built on trusting the Lord and knowing He will be with me through the good and the bad times. If not for you, and for Hank, of course, I could have walked right up to that package and picked it up. But I didn't do that. Same goes for the times when I was shot at and missed."

"Meaning my wife's murder could have been prevented."

"I didn't say that. I've already told you I don't know why bad things happen to good people. I do know we all have choices and

those choices have consequences. But I also
know that there are times when we can't win
no matter how hard we try. If I were running
the universe nobody would ever die. They'd all
live happily ever after, like characters in a fairy
tale. All pets would live forever, too. But this
earth would get awfully crowded awfully fast."

"Is that supposed to be funny?" Caleb was
frowning at her.

"Pragmatic," Vivienne said. Sweeping the
spectators with a glance, she shouldered past
him and started for the ambulance.

Her glance rose to the upper portion of her
apartment building, then traveled across the
street to a similar structure that shaded and
closed in the street as if it were a canyon made
of steel and stone.

Sighing, she quoted part of the twenty-third
Psalm. "'Yea, though I walk through the val-
ley of the shadow of death...'"

Caleb came up close behind. "What did you
say?"

Rather than answer directly Vivienne continued. "'Thy rod and thy staff they comfort me,'"
she said, then turned a smile on him and added,
"The FBI agent makes a nice addition, too."


Spotting Gavin Sutherland among the re-
sponders, Caleb motioned him over while

paramedics checked Vivienne. "You're a long way from the K-9 unit. How'd you get here so fast?"

Sutherland nodded. "I was in the area, actually, for a meeting when the call came in. I was definitely right about the safe house."

"About that. I'm not sure the safe-house-sharing business is going to work, Sergeant. Your K-9 officer is too hardheaded."

To Caleb's chagrin, Gavin chuckled. "You don't say."

"I do say. If she hadn't been worried about her dog I suspect she would have grabbed that box before it started smoking and we wouldn't be having this conversation."

"Nonsense. Vivienne Armstrong is one of my most reliable officers."

"Then I take back all the compliments I gave your unit," Caleb said, tamping down his temper. "That woman believes she's invincible."

"I doubt that very much," Gavin replied. "My team knows we're not bulletproof."

"That's not how it looks to me."

Frowning, Gavin asked, "Are you saying *you're* the one in charge of whether somebody lives or dies? That's pretty bold."

Frustrated, Caleb threw up his hands. "If we can't make a difference, why bother coming to work at all?"

"I understand you're speaking from personal experience." Gavin clapped Caleb on the shoulder and leaned in to converse privately. "Look. If I had all the answers I'd be glad to share them. I don't. None of us do. It's not our job to promise a guaranteed outcome. It's our job to do what we've been trained for, to the best of our abilities, and leave the rest to our heavenly Father."

"Even if we don't agree with the end result?"

"Especially if we don't," Gavin said, sighing and nodding. "Especially if we don't."

Vivienne wasn't concerned for herself. It was Hank's health that worried her. She knew that smoke from burning plastic could be lethal—she just wasn't sure whether or not toxic fumes had reached her beloved K-9.

She allowed the medics to flush out her eyes only after they had taken care of her four-footed partner. Thankfully he wasn't acting as if he was ill or in pain.

Caleb had paused a short distance away to speak with her boss and she was pretty sure they were discussing her. That was good since she seemed to be under siege. It was much easier to bravely face aggression when it was directed against strangers and all she had to do was intercede on their behalf, which was likely

the way the FBI agent felt about her. They really didn't know much about each other besides the intersection of their jobs.

That conclusion brought her up short. She knew far more about what made Caleb Black tick than he did about her. Trauma wasn't a big part of her story. She'd basically had a happy childhood, followed by college courses in law enforcement and specialized training with K-9 units. The moment she'd begun working with Hank she'd known she'd found her calling.

Sooty and looking weary, Caleb joined her. He saluted with a bottle of cold water. "Have you had anything to drink?"

"Not yet."

Presented with the bottle he'd been drinking out of, she didn't hesitate to accept. Normally she didn't share food or beverages, but in his case an exception was easy. "Thanks."

"Welcome. How's the pooch?"

Vivienne smiled. "As you can see, he's fine and raring to go again."

"What do you think about using him to check the hallway by your room? He is the main reason you stopped on the stairs, right?"

"Right. His training is search and rescue, not explosives, so another K-9 might do a better job." She scanned the surroundings, looking for her boss, then pointed. "I need to ask Sarge

if he's sending Henry Roarke and his bomb-detection beagle, Cody. That's what I'd do."

It wasn't a surprise to hear Caleb chuckle. "You really like to run things, don't you?"

A smile quirked and her watery eyes focused on him. "I like to see things done properly, that's all."

He returned her grin. "Well, I hate to break this to you but nothing has changed about going to the safe house except what you get to bring. The crime-scene techs will be going over your apartment and that hallway for hours yet. What do you say we go check out our new digs and see what we need?"

With a sign of resignation, Vivienne agreed. "All right. Maybe we'll have to go shopping."

"There's bound to be some extra clothing at the house so don't worry about that."

"Aw. I was looking forward to picking up new outfits."

Judging by the way he rolled his eyes he was expecting a marathon shopping trip. Well, she'd fool him. Generally speaking, she spent more time picking out a dog toy than she did a summer outfit. Shorts and T-shirts were her go-to choices and simple flip-flops would do for shoes. Too bad she hadn't left a jogging outfit at the station.

Vivienne led the way to Gavin and watched

Caleb nod when the sergeant told her exactly the same thing. She gave up. "Okay. You win. I'll go to the safe house now. Might as well since I have no home anymore."

A twinge of regret passed quickly as reality became clearer. If there had been any question about what she should do next, circumstances had ended that debate. The safe house awaited. So did her assigned guardian, although she wished she knew whether or not he truly objected to sticking so close to her. Personally, she kind of liked knowing he'd be there if she needed him.

Warmth flooded her cheeks and she bowed her head to hide the telling reaction. Any ideas she'd had about squelching her feelings regarding Caleb Black may as well be discarded. They were going to be forced to share a dwelling in spite of her misgivings and there wasn't a thing she could do to stop it, so she would try to enjoy it…but only a little.

That much mandated togetherness could certainly complicate her life, she concluded, thinking of the way her emotions had so quickly connected her to him.

She sneaked a peek and found him studying her as if she was the face on a Wanted poster. She boldly met and held his gaze. "What?"

His brow furrowed, eyes narrowing. "You like the idea."

"What are you talking about?"

"Me. You. The safe house. You think it's funny that I got stuck with you and your dog."

*Well, that hurt!* Vivienne managed to laugh. "It's only funny if we look on the bright side, Agent Black. Hank will love having a yard to play in, even if it's a little one. And I won't have to duck every time I step out the door."

"What about my task of babysitting? What's funny about that?"

"Not much. You're a pretty serious guy." She flashed a smile. "Maybe Hank and I can teach you how to loosen up and have a little fun."

"When I'm not busy saving your life, you mean?"

Subdued, Vivienne said, "Yeah. When nobody is trying to shoot me or blow me to bits."

# ELEVEN

Brooklyn Heights was fairly quiet as Caleb cruised slowly past the designated safe house and used the electronic opener to raise the garage door. On the second pass he pulled up the narrow drive and into the garage, closing the door as soon as his SUV was clear.

Seated beside him, Vivienne had been silent during the ride. Hank gave a bark that sounded excited. Only then did she stir.

Caleb joined her as she liberated her K-9 from the rear cargo section. "Let me get his food and things for you."

"I want to see the house first," Vivienne said.

"This is the only one in Brooklyn that has any kind of yard," Caleb told her, "just in case you were thinking of rejecting it."

"I never said that."

"You didn't have to." He pulled a tagged

key from his pocket and unlocked the door between the garage and house, then stood back.

"Aren't you going to go first and clear it?"

"That was done a few minutes before we arrived. But if you want me to…"

"Of course not. Besides, Hank will tell me if there's a problem."

"I've been meaning to ask you more about that," Caleb said. He followed her into the pristine kitchen. Everything except the beige tiled floor was white, which gave the room a sterile feel. It was, however, nice to be able to tell how spotless the cleaning crew had left it and the light citrus scent was pleasing.

"This, of course, is the kitchen," he said, making conversation because the silence was uncomfortable.

"Could have fooled me. I always keep my stove in the bedroom."

He chose to play along with her sarcasm. "Mine's in the garage. Then if I burn dinner the smoke alarm doesn't go off."

"Very sensible," she said as she made her way across the compact living room. "We may want to throw a sheet or blanket over the sofa. Whoever chose burgundy velour didn't have a dog with white hair."

"Okay. Let's see if we can find a linen closet." He followed her down the hallway. "There

are two bedrooms, two baths and bars on the windows for security."

"Perfect," she said.

Caleb agreed. Vivienne Armstrong was the kind of person who knew how to roll with the punches. Very few of his acquaintances shared her strength of character, let alone her sunny outlook. In a way he envied her the joy she seemed to carry with her and so freely share, yet he knew his heart would never accept such a rosy attitude.

Dark thoughts plagued him daily, so much so that he had become comfortable with them. Was that why he presently felt uneasy? For the first time in seven years, was he starting to question his mode of grieving? Experts taught that there were steps of grief to pass through and deal with. He knew that. He also knew that no two people handled loss the exact same way. Who was to say he was wrong to keep the memory of his family alive as he did? What else did he have?

Ahead of him, Vivienne passed through an open doorway and into the last bedroom. It was decorated very much like an average hotel room, as was the entire house. Heavy brocade drapes covered the single window, there was a television opposite the double bed and a digital clock radio on an end table.

"I'll take this one if you don't mind," she said. "It gives me room for Hank's portable kennel."

"I thought he stayed loose all the time when he was at home."

She smiled. "He does, unless I need him confined for some reason. We try to prepare for all eventualities and sometimes I need a break from all that canine enthusiasm."

"Right. While you look for an extra sheet to protect the couch I'll check the kitchen and see if we have enough food. I assume the crew that prepped the house took care of stocking the refrigerator, but there may be a few things you'd like that we don't have."

"Don't bother. I'm an easy keeper."

"A what?"

"Haven't you ever heard that term? It applies to animals that stay healthy and happy while eating whatever is provided and never demand more. They're easy to keep."

"Okay, then let's go get Hank's gear from my car and set you two up."

Hearing his name, the border collie pranced and circled at the end of his leash. Vivienne laughed. "I'm going to take him out in the fenced yard and make sure it's secure while you do that. He really needs exercise."

"I'll come with you."

She made a grumpy face, then modified it with a lopsided grin before she said, "I wonder if they make a kennel big enough for overly enthusiastic FBI agents."

"You'd never talk me into crawling inside so don't even try," Caleb countered. "I promise I'll stand down as soon as we've both inspected the premises."

"I will believe that when I see it." By this time she was grinning at him. "What happened to trusting the prep crew?"

Staying serious was impossible in the face of her amusement, but he did manage to temper his smile when he said, "One of us has to stay alert twenty-four-seven."

"I'll leave that to Hank." She gently patted his silky fur. "C'mon, guys. Let's see what the grass looks like out back."

He'd made certain they hadn't been followed to the safe house, yet Caleb tensed as he preceded her out the door. There was nothing fancy about the postage-stamp-size yard, but it was neatly mowed and edged against a block wall on one side, with six-foot-high, rough-cut, cedar planks on the other and at the rear. The only exit besides through the house was a narrow metal gate on the east side that was secured with a heavy chain and padlock.

In a defensive mindset, he checked neigh-

boring houses and noted that none provided a clear view of the enclosed yard. That was a plus. So was the lack of easy access from outside.

While Vivienne led Hank along the perimeter on a leash, presumably to examine the fence, Caleb strode to the gate and inspected the lock and chain, finding it more than adequate. All was well.

He paused to watch her and marveled at the way she took everything in stride. No matter what happened she seemed to be content— once she'd voiced her opinion, at least. That thought made him smile. Part of her charm was the way she stood up for herself and had the courage to question authority. It probably drove her boss up the wall, but Caleb admired her for it. To a point.

An unexplained shiver shot up his spine despite the warm evening. Logic contradicted instinct. He chose to listen to the latter. "Let's go get the dog's stuff. I'm starving and unless you plan to cook, I'm going to fix us something."

Vivienne was grinning as she returned to him with Hank at her heels. "How does peanut butter and jelly sound?"

"Meager. Why?"

"Because I don't cook much for myself and

that's my favorite recipe. If I want to make a fancy meal I use jam."

Caleb had to laugh. "That settles it. I'll cook." He had already shed his suit coat. Now he rolled up the sleeves of his dress shirt. "The garage is locked so it's safe for you to bring in the kennel and food. Unless you want my help."

To his chagrin, she assured him she could manage alone. It had taken monumental effort to offer to let her do it without him. He wanted to be there. To guard and guide her despite her off-putting attitude toward accepting help. But *his* attitude made no sense. She was currently armed, as well as accompanied by a trained K-9. She really didn't need him to hover over her so why did he feel such a strong urge to keep doing it?

A sudden realization hit him like a base-ball bat to the side of his head. Genuine need was there, of course, but the unquenchable desire to protect came from inside him. When he'd looked at Vivienne in the past he'd seen a shadow of Maggie. Heard gunshots. Felt the bullets pierce his heart.

He was well aware that Vivienne wasn't Maggie; the K-9 officer was very much her own person and he saw her for who she was. Somehow, in an astonishingly brief length of

time, he'd managed to let go of his tragic past enough to begin to focus on the present. And perhaps the future, he added to himself. That notion did not sit well. Not well, at all.

Vivienne had felt a shift in the overall atmosphere in the safe house. Any change would have worried her if Hank had acted nervous. Since the K-9 was calm, she was, too. Puzzled, but calm.

Whatever Caleb was cooking smelled heavenly. "How about I set the table?"

"Good idea. I would have asked you to but I figured if I did, you'd argue against it."

She rolled her eyes and struck a theatrical pose. "Oh, please. I am not that bad. I'm just used to handling life by myself and making my own decisions. There's nothing wrong with being independent."

"Not if you add a big dose of logic." He gestured at the pan sizzling on the stove. "It's like cooking. Leave out a key ingredient and the dish may not be edible."

"You *have* heard about my cooking!"

"Hey, I'm trying to be serious here."

She capitulated as she reached into an upper cupboard for two plates. "Sorry. I get it. I really do. It's just hard for me to admit I need

help with anything. I've always taken care of myself."

"Not as a child, I assume."

Heaving a noisy sigh, she shrugged. "Not entirely, no. My parents weren't neglectful the way Penny and Bradley say theirs were. Mine just spent a lot of time working and earning enough to keep us in a nice house and provide all the extras. There were times I did wish they were at home more, particularly my mother."

"You weren't an only child," Caleb remarked without turning to watch her.

"I might as well have been." Another sigh. "My brother was a freshman in college by the time I was born. I decided early that I wanted a big family. Big and noisy like some of my friends' and filling the house with love. Sometimes it was so quiet in my childhood home it was eerie."

She left the plates on the small dinette table and returned for silverware. "How about you? Do you have siblings?"

"Nope. After we lost my dad, I was old enough to be out on my own and my mother was free to go live with her sister in Pennsylvania."

"I'm sorry about your dad," Vivienne said.

Sneaking a peek at his hand as he stirred a pot of spaghetti sauce, she noted that his wed-

ding ring was still in place on his left ring finger. In his heart he was married. Period. Nothing was going to change that.

She couldn't help admiring him for keeping his vows, even now. That kind of love and dedication was rare and precious.

Vivienne almost—*almost*—huffed as her imagination took her deduction one step further. The man was miserable, lonely and wasting God-given years, years that he could be enjoying, at least in some regard, despite his horrific loss. And he thought *she* was the stubborn one? Ha! Caleb Black put her meager resistance to change in the minor leagues. He was by far the champ.

She didn't notice that he had turned until he said, "You look funny."

*No doubt.* "Funny as in laughable or funny as in strange?"

Shaking his head, he held the long-handled spoon over his cupped hand so it wouldn't drip spaghetti sauce on the floor. "Beats me. I don't know you well enough to judge. You aren't planning on skipping out on me, are you?"

"Not a chance. I've had a long talk with myself and I can see what a big mistake that would be."

"You talk to yourself?"

"Hey, you're the profiler. Doesn't everybody do that?"

"Not and expect a sensible conclusion," Caleb said.

Vivienne smiled over at him. "Not everybody has an invisible target on her back, either. I intend to stay alive to make the best of my life and I don't plan to fight the one person God is apparently using to defend me."

"I told you. I don't call myself a Christian anymore."

Her smile widened. "That's okay. You're still in the game whether you believe it or not."

# TWELVE

Caleb barely tasted his meal. Few people had the ability to see past confusing circumstances and pinpoint the crux of a problem the way Vivienne did. When she'd insisted he was still being used for good, he had to agree, at least in principle. That had been his goal from the beginning. And yet, when she'd expressed that same concept he'd seen it from a different angle.

Suppose God hadn't deserted him. Suppose Caleb was the one who had turned his back. All he had to do was… What? Accept the loss of his hopes and dreams? Forgive himself for not saving his wife and their baby? Forgive God for not stepping in and stopping that fatal bullet?

His jaw set as he glanced at Vivienne across the kitchen table. She smiled back at him, then sobered when she saw his expression. "Have

you been sucking on a lemon again? You sure look like it."

Caleb didn't want her to know what he was thinking. He refrained, as much to avoid an in-depth conversation as to protect her feelings. "It's been a rough day."

"Um, yeah. I noticed."

She laid her fork on her plate. "Dinner was delicious. Thank you."

"It was nothing, really."

He stood, picked up his half-eaten dinner and reached toward her plate.

She also got to her feet but didn't hand him her dirty dish. "You cooked so I'll clean up."

"Fine."

"No argument? No specific rules for washing the dishes? I'm disappointed."

He managed a smile. "You're the one who keeps trying to run things. So the cleanup is all yours. Have at it."

"What a guy," she said with a smirk. "Just when I thought you weren't going to let me do anything my way you change your tune and turn KP over to me. Thanks, FBI."

He huffed. "Don't celebrate too much. There's a dishwasher next to the sink. All you'll need to do is scrub a couple of pans."

"And feed my dog," Vivienne said. "Hank comes first."

As if to prove the point, the border collie tagged along to the sink and sat obediently next to her. Vivienne smiled at him fondly. "Yes, Hank. Your dinner is coming. I promise."

Watching the officer and her K-9, Caleb had to admit they had an amazing rapport. Her brown eyes sparkled. Her smile telegraphed gentle affection along with command. And Hank's gaze never wavered from hers as long as she was looking at him.

When he saw her lift a long string of pasta and dangle it over the dog's nose, he had to grin. They had apparently played this game before because Hank held his position, quivering and licking his lips but making no effort to lunge for the treat.

She finally said, "Take it," and the pasta disappeared in a blur.

"Finally," Caleb said. "I thought you were going to wait so long your poor dog drooled himself to death."

Vivienne laughed. "I'm not supposed to give him anything but his regulation dog food. I just can't resist adding a special treat once in a while."

"I'm astounded!" Caleb said, with an exaggerated reaction. "You broke a rule?"

"Don't you dare tell," she warned before

chuckling again. "I have a reputation for perfection to protect."

He smiled again. "I don't doubt that for a second, as long as everybody else does things your way."

"Now you're catching on," she teased. "I knew you were smart."

"Being sequestered here with you and your K-9 is harder than I thought it would be," he said...very honestly. Suddenly he felt the need to come up with an excuse for what he'd just said. "It's not exactly conducive to working."

"Why not?" She was facing him, hands fisted on her hips. "We won't bother you one bit. Put your computer on the dining table and go at it. Hank and I will finish here and take a stroll around the backyard."

Caleb felt his brow begin to knit. He cast her a glance meant to warn as he said, "Inside the fence. Stay inside the fence, where you can't be seen."

"Now who's giving orders?" she countered, softening the retort with a soft laugh.

His need to protect her was stronger than he was. "I am."

"So you are. And since you happen to be right, I'll gladly promise to keep Hank in the yard."

"Thank you for that," he said.

Caleb was set up on the table as she'd suggested by the time she'd loaded the dishwasher and fed the dog. He'd hung his shoulder holster on the back of his chair and was keeping an eye on her surreptitiously. When she started down the hallway instead of heading for the back door, he asked, "Where are you going?"

"To find the extra clothing you told me about. I'd just as soon not get my uniform dirty until I know I can get a fresh one."

"Always taking chances," Caleb teased. "You just ate spaghetti while wearing your uniform."

"I know. And did dishes." Vivienne rolled her eyes. "I didn't think of changing until dinner was on the table and didn't want to hurt your feelings by being late."

"You actually thought of that? Incredible."

That brought another laugh. "You're just now discovering I'm different? Boy, you must be overtired."

"It's not being tired," Caleb argued. "It's you. You're not the easiest person to figure out." He'd stopped watching her and was focusing on the laptop, where a multitude of case files awaited. "When you get changed and done with the dog, I want to pick your brain about something."

"My brain? Why?"

"Because of the way you described your childhood," Caleb said. "That's been bothering me ever since you told me about it. I'm sure I'm not the first investigator to wonder if that may be part of the reason the McGregor and Emery parents were killed."

"My mom and dad didn't do drugs or neglect me," Vivienne countered. "They loved me. I know they did."

"Inadequate parents can love their kids deeply," Caleb said. "It's more a matter of them not knowing what's right or not being in a position to give their kids what the rest of us consider proper care and guidance."

"I'd never thought of it that way."

"Maybe we could apply that line of thinking to the possible motives that woman had for abducting the Potter boy. It's obvious his mother was taking good care of him. He was clean and healthy and happy."

"Except for his tears when he was snatched," Vivienne added. "I'd also like to figure out how one person could have done all that woman did and still take shots at me after the kidnapping attempt was foiled. I suspect she may have a partner in crime."

"That's definitely possible." He took pains to keep from looking at her because he feared his concern would show. "Go get changed and

take care of your K-9. We can talk more about your case later."

"Okay. See ya."

Judging by her lighthearted-sounding reply, she wasn't too worried. That, alone, worried him more than if she had been wringing her hands and trembling with fright—which he couldn't imagine Vivienne Armstrong ever doing.

Before he realized what *he* was doing, Caleb whispered, "Father, protect her."

He stared at the computer screen, seeing nothing but his own reflection. What made him think his prayers would be heard, let alone answered? Nothing did, he realized, reaching out again with his mind. He might not be connected to God, but clearly Vivienne was, so why not pray for her safety? It couldn't hurt and there was the outside possibility it might help.

That alone was enough reason to try.

The clothing Vivienne found in the bedroom closets and dressers was adequate. Size wasn't really a problem, either, since a variety had been provided, so she donned running shorts and a tank top. She thought about laying out something casual for Caleb, then decided against it. He was a big boy. He could take care

of himself, at least on a physical plane. Emotionally, not so much.

Suddenly, her alert K-9 stiffened, his hackles raised, and focused on the window. A low growl echoed in the small room.

Vivienne held out a hand to signal *stop* and crept past Hank. Blinds behind heavy drapes covered the inside of the window. She parted the fabric just enough to reach the slats in the white plastic blinds and part them with her fingertips. The trembling of her whole body made peering out more difficult, but she managed to see enough to know the threat was real. A shadowy figure emerged from the bushes and made a dash for the street.

Whirling, Vivienne raced back toward the living room. All she said was "Prowler" as she grabbed for her discarded sidearm.

That was enough to animate Caleb. He beat her to the front door and jerked it open, gun in hand, then took a shooter's stance on the porch, obviously ready to fire if necessary.

The yard was empty when Vivienne joined him seconds later. Cars continued to pass in the street but nobody was close to the house itself. "Left. He ran left," she said, almost shouting.

Caleb stopped her with an extended arm. "Stay here and watch my back."

If the order hadn't been the most sensible choice she might have balked. As things stood, the agent was making more sense than she was, considering her vulnerability standing there on the porch with Hank. She crouched. Kept Caleb in sight until he swung around the corner to where the locked gate was. Her heart was pounding so loud, so rapidly, she was sure her K-9 could hear every beat.

The moment Caleb reappeared, she took a deep breath and blew it out noisily, then asked, "Nothing?"

"Nothing. Are you sure you saw somebody?"

She was miffed and let it show. "Yes, I'm sure. I don't have to imagine threats. There are plenty of real ones around these days."

"Okay. I had to ask, though. Were you able to see a face?"

Vivienne pouted theatrically. "No. But there was a prowler. Right at my window." She edged down the porch steps, staying alert but lowering her gun to her side. "Look at the bushes. You can tell somebody went through them. See?"

"I do. Too bad it isn't safe for Hank to trail the person."

"Who says?"

"I do. Your sergeant agrees, if you'll recall.

He's ordered you to stay out of sight. That's what we're doing here."

"And Hank won't work for you," Vivienne added with a frown and a shrug. "Okay. Let's go back inside before we attract too much attention."

"Right. The backyard is safer."

"When you're right, you're right," she said. "Go check it if you want to. I'm going to strap on some of my gear before I join you."

Watching Caleb leave, she couldn't help feeling thankful for his presence. He might be the most cantankerous partner she'd ever had, but he kept his head no matter what was going on around them. That was a virtue she valued beyond words.

Caleb patrolled the perimeter of the rear yard as if he was stalking an armed killer. *Which I might be*, he told himself. He had no doubt that Vivienne had spotted an interloper and under other circumstances he would have chalked it up to curious kids or nosy neighbors. However, given their current dilemma and the fact they knew so little about the threats to her life, he had to assume the worst.

"I hope she does the same," he muttered as he returned to the house. She was waiting in the kitchen with Hank at her side. To Caleb's

delight both she and the dog seemed glad to see him.

"All clear," he said, eyeing her filled holster. "I'm glad you've decided to stay armed. Can't be too careful."

"Or too paranoid," she said wryly. "I'm beginning to feel for the partners of the attack and protection K-9s. This is a bit more action than I'm used to."

Caleb opened the door for her, then followed into the yard. "There's usually a lot of paperwork and desk time to my job, too," he said. "With less adrenaline."

That brought a slight smile and she nodded.

"Since the safe house has been compromised—and we have to assume the prowler wasn't random—I'm calling my boss to get us moved." At her nod, he made the call, dismayed to hear there were no other safe houses available tonight. At least a patrol car would be monitoring until morning. It wasn't enough, but he'd take what he could get.

Once they saw a patrol car parking out front Caleb relaxed…just a bit.

"Getting back to what we were talking about," Vivienne said, "boredom can have its upside. Why don't you have a seat on the steps while I exercise Hank. You can keep an eye on us from there and he won't be so distracted."

"You're sure?"

"Positive," she replied. "We all need to dial down the angst or we'll be too exhausted to be at our best."

Caleb nodded, then smiled at her. "There are moments when you actually make sense," he teased.

Vivienne's responding silly face showed that she got the joke. So did saying, "Stick around and I'll show you just how smart I can be, FBI."

After putting Hank through his paces, she let him off his leash to explore at will. The sun was setting. Fireflies blinked near the bushes as they rose in the cooler air. Their season was nearly over yet they continued to flash green, looking for a mate, never giving up as long as they lived.

She would do well to take a lesson from the insects, Vivienne told herself. Even if she got too old to have children of her own she could foster or adopt later in life. It didn't matter whether or not she ever found the perfect husband.

That conclusion took her immediately to thoughts of Caleb Black and she darted a quick glance his way. *No, no, no! Not him. Anybody but him.* And yet...

Sighing and lifting her eyes and thoughts to

heaven, she tried to picture the kind of man she wanted. "Father, you promised to supply all our needs."

*Whoa!* The difference hit her hard. *Needs, not wants.* So did she truly need an emotionally wounded person like Caleb? Did he need a new life partner despite his resistance to even consider it? In this case, she was delighted to turn the answers over to the Lord and let Him take charge. *Sort of.*

The added disclaimer made her smile and look again to the source of her strength and peace. "Help me do the right thing, please, Father? And not get in Your way too much."

What she yearned for was both understanding and acceptance, no matter what happened. That was a lot to ask for. And it was a lot to expect from herself. The habit of questioning authority in her workplace clearly bled over into her prayer life and that was not good. Human nature, but not good.

A bit disgusted with herself and tired of self-analysis, she opted to go back inside. "Hank. Come," she called, starting for the porch.

He stopped sniffing, raised his head and looked at her.

"Hank?"

The border collie's tail was wagging slowly. She watched his attention go from her to the

side gate, then come back. Was their earlier intruder out there again? "Caleb?" she began, expressing her thoughts via a sidelong glance she was hoping he'd understand. Judging by the way he tensed and rose slowly, deliberately, he'd gotten her message.

Caleb crooked a finger at her, his gun in his other hand. "Come here."

She approached. He leaned closer as she passed. "Inside. The dog, too."

"No. I can back you up," she whispered.

The stare he focused on her had her reconsider; he *needed* to protect her, but he had to remember that she was a cop and a good one. Pride insisted that she ignore him and stand her ground. Worried that an argument might interfere with good judgment on both their parts, she chose to open the door. "Hank. Come."

Vivienne was through the doorway in seconds. To her relief, Caleb soon followed. He holstered his weapon. "I didn't see anybody, but that doesn't mean they weren't there and slipped past the patrol. Maybe we should keep trying to find another place to stay."

"There's nowhere else to go that makes sense. A hotel could put others in danger. Besides, there's a cop parked right out front and with both of us armed here inside we have the

upper hand. I'm perfectly capable of backing you up, you know."

Caleb retreated. "Don't."

"Don't what?"

"Don't even think of putting yourself in harm's way to protect me."

*Of course.* Vivienne flashed back to his sad story. His late wife had been trying to outwit a killer and had paid the ultimate price. *Can he be right? Would I do the same?* she asked herself.

To admit it aloud would be unwise. To let herself accept the truth of the premise, however, was just as foolish. Putting her life on the line for strangers had become almost a daily occurrence. That was part of the job. But sticking her neck out beyond her sworn duty was different and that was exactly what Caleb was warning against.

Nevertheless, she knew the answer to her own question. Would she risk everything to help him, to protect him?

In her heart the truth was crystal clear. Not only would she defend him with every ability she possessed, but she was also eager to do so. There might be no such thing as love at first sight, but something had come over her in the short length of time she and Caleb Black had

been thrown together. If she ever figured out how she felt and why, she might even tell him.

A heaviness descended over Vivienne. Imagining either of them losing a chance to find out if they belonged together was one of the saddest ideas she'd ever had. She had to take care of him, to see that he came out of this alive and well. Whether he liked it or not.

# THIRTEEN

"Ice cream?" Caleb looked up from his computer as Vivienne joined him. "Now?"

"Think of it as medicine. Any woman will tell you it can cure just about anything."

"Even criminals' need to get revenge?" He waited, expecting a contradiction.

"Maybe not that. I still plan to polish off this pint." She frowned. "I am sorry I reminded you of a terrible time in your past."

Before he could come up with a platitude or change the subject, Vivienne licked the spoon and said, "I know it's impossible to stop that from happening, but I promise to do my best to avoid reminding you of your late wife."

Caleb was slowly shaking his head as he leaned back, away from the table holding his laptop. "That's not going to work."

"Why not?" she asked, taking another spoonful of ice cream.

"Because you're a lot like her. It's not your

hair or eyes or anything like that. It's what's inside, what makes you tick."

"Is that so bad?"

Watching her for clues to underlying secrets, he shrugged. "So how many times did you run away from home?"

Her jaw dropped. Moments passed.

"Wow. You are a profiler!"

"Told you. You did tell me you weren't neglected but that you had a lonely childhood." He straightened in the chair and turned back to his computer. "I got to thinking about this when I was going over the murder files looking for similarities. Both Penelope McGregor and Lucy Emery were in day-care facilities that had extended hours, most days for fourteen, sixteen hours a day. I'm not saying there's anything wrong with day care—it's a necessity for working parents. But the extended hours struck me. Both sets of parents were barely part of the children's lives. I wonder if the killer—or killers—saw himself as a vigilante who had been similarly treated." He shrugged. "I keep coming back to that. There's not much personal info about Randall Gage in his file. But why would he have targeted the McGregors when there was no other connection between them? Why spare the child? Why give the child a stuffed toy?"

Vivienne nodded. "Talk to my sergeant about your theory in the morning," she said. "And my colleague, K-9 officer Belle Montera's fiancé, Emmett Gage, might be able to offer some insight into his cousin's upbringing. I don't think he and Randall Gage were close, but Emmett could have some information."

He nodded, taking notes as she spoke.

"And by the way, I was never mad at my parents," Vivienne insisted.

"Are you close to them now?"

The lack of a quick answer told him all he needed to know about her thoughts on the subject. "It's not bad to pull away from destructive personality types," Caleb said. "You just don't intend to let anybody else hurt you."

"Nobody wants that."

Caleb could tell she was getting upset so he dialed back his profile of her. "I overheard you telling Penny McGregor that you want a big family, lots of kids. Is that right?"

"Yes. So?"

"So is that really what you want or are you hoping to repair the damage your absent parents did by opening your home and heart to a bunch of kids in need and loving them all?"

Ignoring her gaping mouth and widening eyes, Caleb went on. "This may be why you haven't found a husband."

Her jaw snapped shut, eyebrows arching. "I beg your pardon."

"Being cautious about choosing a mate isn't a fault, Vivienne. It's a virtue. You're brave about everything else. Ask yourself if it's not high time you showed courage about dating."

"Me? What about you?"

He frowned. "We're not talking about me."

"Well, maybe we should be."

Raising both hands, Caleb made the sign of a *T*. "Time-out. I apologize for profiling you when that's not what we're here for."

Flashes of conflicting emotions passed across her face, ending when she took a deep, settling breath and let it out with a whoosh. "Okay. I forgive you. Sort of." She made a face. "So what do you think about the Potter boy's kidnapper? Having met the mother, Susanna, and Jake, I doubt his abductor did it because she thought he'd been neglected."

"You're absolutely right. I've been researching local disappearances of other male toddlers but haven't come up with any new leads. That's one reason I suspect a mental illness that may be long-standing. If the woman who snatched Jake experienced the loss of a child, no matter when it happened, she may be stuck in a time warp and be trying to replace a baby she lost

years ago. That gives us far too many possibilities to check out."

"So what else can we do?"

"I think we should start by talking to Mrs. Potter one more time, the way we'd planned. I have a transcript of her previous interview from right after the abduction, but that doesn't show me everything I can deduce in a face-to-face meeting. Sometimes it's not so much what a person says as the way they say it."

"My K-9 liked her."

Caleb had to laugh. "That's your criteria?"

"It's a start," Vivienne said. "I'd sooner trust the opinion of this dog than half the people I know."

"Amen to that," he said without thinking, then sought to redirect her. "Your ice cream is melting."

"Guess I'll have to hurry and eat the whole carton, then, huh? What a shame. I was planning on offering some to you."

"Let me at that ice cream," he said.

She laughed and handed him a spoon. He had to admit it felt good that they were "okay" again.

If Vivienne hadn't been bone-tired she might have had more trouble sleeping. The presence of Hank, curled up at the foot of the bed, did have a calming effect. Yes, he was going to

get spoiled and probably need extra refresher training, but that wasn't the end of the world. All the K-9s and handlers went through mandated repetitions, although not necessarily for the same reasons.

She awoke before morning. Hank growled. He was standing at the foot of the mattress, staring at the window, illuminated by light from the motion sensors in the front yard. Someone was outside.

Heart racing, Vivienne reached for her holster and drew her gun. Knowing that nobody could get to her through that barred window wasn't enough. She had to meet possible threats head-on. Police training was useless if she failed to use it.

Hank never moved from the bed, but his focus did shift from the outside to inside. Soon, he was staring at the closed and locked bedroom door. His growling deepened. The doorknob started to move, to turn slightly. Then something rattled at the window and the dog's attention changed.

Vivienne didn't know which threat to respond to first. Hank seemed concerned about both areas, but did either pose danger? She edged toward the window without turning on the lights. The room was small enough to navigate in near darkness and she didn't want to

silhouette herself against the blinds. A sharp rap on her door made her jump. Hank barked ferociously.

"Vivienne?" Caleb called, "Are you all right?"

"Yes." Irrational ire rose. "What are you doing wandering around in the middle of the night scaring me to death?" She pulled on a robe over the extralong man's T-shirt she been sleeping in and belted it.

Unlocking the door and jerking it open, she faced Caleb, her gun pointed at the ceiling, the safety on.

"I thought I heard something outside," he said.

Ah, so it was Caleb who'd set off the motion sensors. "Yeah, so did Hank. You. Why did you go outside?"

She saw the muscles in his jaw clenching. His posture gave new meaning to the definition of "tense." When he said, "I haven't been outside," she felt her heart race.

"You haven't?"

"No." Peering past her, Caleb studied the K-9. Hank was still concentrating on the barred window. "Stay here. I'm going to check the yard."

"I'm going with you."

"No. You are not," Caleb said firmly.

She knew where his overprotectiveness was coming from, but he had to get it through his stubborn head that she was a police officer.

"Caleb, I'm a cop. We need to work as a team. The sooner we check to see who or what is bothering Hank, the sooner we can relax."

"I have full respect for your abilities and training, Vivienne. I just—"

He didn't finish his sentence.

She stood firm, shoulders squared. "Let's go, then."

"What about Hank?"

"I want him inside for now so I don't have to worry about him. If we don't find a prowler, I'll harness him to track." Vivienne could tell from the stubborn set of Caleb's jaw that he disagreed once again. Thankfully, he was in too much of a hurry to stop and argue.

The motion-sensor outdoor lights were still activated when Caleb and Vivienne stepped outside. The patrol officer was looking around, shining his flashlight, and let them know he'd hurried over to check front and back when the lights came on, but didn't see anyone. They thanked the officer, who went back to his car.

They searched the yard themselves—no sign of the intruder—and then went back inside.

"Whoever they were, they were scared off," Caleb concluded.

"So now what?"

The tremor in Vivienne's voice touched his heart. Courage was shown by pushing ahead despite normal fear and he had to admire her for it. "Now, I guess we go back to sleep," he said.

"Is that what you plan to do?"

"Probably."

"Meet me in the kitchen instead."

"Why?" Caleb asked. "Is there another pint of ice cream calling your name?"

"Something like that. I may make hot chocolate if we have the ingredients."

He glanced at the clock on the wall. "It's barely five in the morning. We need to sleep more."

"Speak for yourself, FBI. Hank and I are both wide awake and I don't intend to just lie there and stare at the ceiling. I need chocolate. Or maybe just coffee. A lot of coffee."

"And company?" Caleb asked.

"And company," Vivienne admitted. "Know any FBI agents who'd like to join me?"

"I can think of one."

"Good. Give me five minutes. I'm not going to hang around in this ugly robe."

He had to chuckle. He palmed his cell phone and called Gavin Sutherland's private number.

"It's five a.m. This better be important" replaced a standard hello.

"It is," Caleb said. "I can't talk long. Just wanted you to know we've had two more indications that a prowler was outside."

"Are you both all right? The K-9, too?"

"Yes. For a tracking dog he sure has a lot of other useful tricks. He's usually the first one to alert to anything unusual."

"That may be advantageous now, but when he's working he's not supposed to be easily distracted. You're probably ruining a good dog."

"If it keeps Vivienne alive and well, it's worth it," Caleb countered. "Considering all the trouble we've faced since we got here, I suggest you bring her and Hank back into regular service and let them work while I try to come up with a safer place for them to stay."

"Speaking of sticking around, what are your plans? Have you interviewed the Potter woman again? And what about finishing those profiles we need?"

"I'm close to making a report about the murders," Caleb assured him. "In the meantime, I'll stick to Vivienne—I mean Officer Armstrong—like a bulletproof shield."

"You do that," Gavin said. "See you in a few hours."

Caleb was lowering his phone when Vivienne reappeared. His breath caught. Before, she'd been a jogger or a police officer in uniform. Now she looked so feminine he hardly recognized her. She wore a tank top with a ruffle at the neck and a knee-length flippy skirt.

Rather than sound too serious, he quipped, "How do you do, ma'am. I don't believe we've met."

But Vivienne was looking at what he still held—his cell phone. "I didn't hear any phones ring."

"Mine's on silent," Caleb said.

"Care to tell me who you were talking to?"

"I reported to your sergeant about the repeat prowler. There's no point in trying to move safe houses this morning if this one was so easily compromised. I'm sure you'll get word from Gavin shortly. I suggested he put you back to work."

"Hooray!"

"Nice outfit."

She turned in a circle, making the skirt swirl gracefully around her knees. "I don't know what came over me. I was reaching for the clothes I wore last night when I saw this in

the closet. Kind of makes me feel like going to church."

"Church?"

"Sure. I felt at home there. Besides, they held a lot of church suppers where a kid like me could get a great meal," she added. "My parents were rarely home so I had to fend for myself."

"You didn't care for the peanut butter sandwiches you told me were your specialty?"

"Not as a steady diet."

He glanced out the window; the sun was just rising. "Now I'm kind of hungry. Bacon and eggs?"

She smiled. "Sounds very good."

He got to work and quickly dished up two plates and put them on the table, then poured coffee for them both and joined her. "Cream or sugar?"

"I'll get it." Jumping up before he could protest, she scanned the counter for a sugar bowl, then went to the refrigerator for the milk she knew was there, bringing both back with her.

Caleb raised a hand to shield his steaming mug. "None for me."

"I know. I remember. Black to match your name. But I may want a second cup. This is so much better than the coffee at work."

"Anything is better than cop coffee."

"Can't argue with you there." She sipped hers, then started on a crisp strip of bacon. "Just the way I like it. A visit to the Potters is first on our agenda for today, right?"

"Right. It's going to be our job to convince her to leave Brooklyn until the kidnapper is caught."

"I'll take Hank along. The little boy loved him."

"Yeah, he did. I was surprised that a working K-9 was so friendly with civilians."

"It's the breed. And Hank's training. He was never taught to be defensive."

She noted Caleb's scowl before he said, "You're kidding."

"No. Why?"

"He's been looking out for you up until now."

"When he alerts it's instinct, not training. He wouldn't hurt a fly, let alone take down an assailant." She paused for emphasis. "Besides, I don't want to see him hurt."

"Of course not." Caleb peeked beneath the table. "Where is he, anyway?"

"Outside. I took a quick look around. It's still secure and the patrol officer is still here."

"Good." A shadow of doubt seemed to fall on Caleb's expression. His green eyes darkened. "Maybe it would be best if you let me

visit Mrs. Potter and the boy by myself. You could catch up on paperwork and stay at the K-9 unit."

"In your dreams," Vivienne countered.

"No, in *Brooklyn*," Caleb joked.

"That is so not funny. Don't even consider leaving me out of this. I was never a target until I stopped that kidnapping. I deserve to be included."

He was shaking his head. "The kidnapper is after you, Vivienne. You've been shot at multiple times. And she, or an accomplice, may even have found you here. She'll stop at nothing until she has some kind of payback for you foiling the kidnapping. Don't you owe it to your unit and to your K-9 to take all necessary precautions?"

"We'll see," she said. "I'll wait until eight to call the station—that's when Gavin arrives. So for now, I'll clean up since you cooked and then take a hot shower and get ready for work."

She cleared their plates, refusing offers of help. He thanked her and headed to the living room with his laptop. She was both glad to have some distance and kind of missed him at the same time.

It was against Vivienne's nature to waste a minute but this morning was the exception. She took her time getting ready, since they

had time to kill. She played with Hank, then prepared for her interview with Mrs. Potter and that sweet little Jake. Finally, she dressed in her uniform and made sure she had everything she needed for work. Then she took a deep breath and headed for the living room… and Caleb Black.

"I'll go take a quick shower myself," he said.

She nodded, then pulled her cell phone out of a pocket and pressed the speed dial for her station. It wasn't exactly 8:00 a.m., when Gavin usually arrived, but it was close enough.

Penny answered. "Brooklyn K-9 Unit. How can I help you?"

"Hi, Penny. It's me, Vivienne. I need to speak with Gavin."

"Sorry. He's not in yet. What's the problem? Is the FBI getting on your nerves?"

Hearing a friendly voice helped immensely. Smiling, Vivienne cradled the phone and spoke quietly, knowing her companion was bound to overhear since he was still in the hallway, but she was unwilling to seek seclusion. Besides, she didn't intend to say anything that needed to be kept from him.

"My last nerve just left," she said. "Gavin told me—us—to interview Susanna Potter today, but a certain FBI agent is trying to keep me out of it."

"I take it he's not succeeding."

"No, he isn't." She raised her glance to meet Caleb's and felt the force of his will zinging up her spine. "I just wanted Gavin to know what was going on in case this agent decides to lock me in a closet or something."

"Is that a possibility?"

She heard Caleb's bedroom door close. "Let's hope not."

Penny chuckled.

"We'll be leaving in around twenty minutes for the Potters'. I'll have my radio, but you can still reach me by phone if you want to keep it private."

"Gotcha." Penelope giggled. "Have a nice day."

Fifteen minutes later, Caleb was back, looking too handsome. "Ready?"

"Ready," she said. "I didn't get to speak to Gavin yet. I'll catch him when I get a chance."

He only nodded at that and they headed out, both of them on red alert. Vivienne didn't see anyone or anything suspicious and Hank was calm. They stopped to let the patrol officer know they were leaving for good and thanked him for helping out.

Vivienne was still wary as she loaded Hank in the back and climbed into the passenger side of the SUV. It didn't help to see Caleb acting

as if they were about to pull out into an active war zone instead of a peaceful neighborhood. "We *will* catch the kidnapper-shooter—and her accomplice if she's working with one. I know we will. She'll trip up. She's already taking too many unnecessary risks," Vivienne insisted.

He glanced at her. "I'm the one who's supposed to predict people's behavior," he said. "But I agree. Luckily, Hank's a great judge of danger. That makes me feel better about your safety."

"Hank is good that way—easy to read. If he growls he's upset. If his tail wags, he's happy. I can't tell from minute to minute what's going on in *your* head."

When he stared at her with those piercing eyes, she wondered even harder what he was thinking.

"You're probably better at reading me than you think," he said. "I wish you weren't, actually," he added with a smile.

Vivienne mirrored his grin. "Think about it this way. Suppose you needed to defend me, as you already are, but I needed to come to your aid, too. You'd be glad I could read you enough to know how to help."

"I don't need anybody's help."

She refused to argue. Time would tell. If and when he decided to unburden himself or

asked for counsel, she'd be there. If he never did, then so be it, but she was going to be terribly disappointed.

It dawned on Vivienne that if she was having this much trouble letting go of her desire to help Caleb, how much worse must it be for him to feel the weight of how he'd lost his wife and baby every moment of every day. It was a wonder he was functional at all, let alone as good at his job as he was.

She purposely changed the subject. "Have you come to any new conclusions about the Potter kidnapping?"

"Suppositions only," he answered. "We know we're dealing with at least one middle-aged woman. She took a young child for no apparent external reason, so chances are she's looking for a replacement for a child she lost or wanted and never had."

"Okay. If she's open to taking any kid, why is she so mad at me for ruining her plans? Jake Potter must have something special about him or she'd just move on to another target."

She knew she'd impressed him when he said, "I agree. I wish I had more to go on, but that's my guess. A lot of what I do utilizes logic and past experience."

"So a lot of the time you're guessing?"

"I'm not crazy about that term, but yes.

Sometimes. It's an educated guess. Just like your conclusion about the kidnapper's motives. The same goes for the profile I've worked out for the McGregor and Emery homicides. Despite the similarities, I think the Emerys were murdered by a copycat—not Randall Gage. Twenty years between the cases? And remember, Gage's DNA wasn't in the system otherwise, so he either hadn't committed other murders or had been careful. He certainly wasn't careful enough at the McGregor house to notice his watch had fallen off."

"Good point," she said, nodding.

"I think he specifically murdered the McGregors, then moved on. And twenty years later, something triggered the copycat, maybe a news report about the decades-old cold case. Of course, I can't be sure, but that's my educated guess."

"Too bad we don't have DNA from the Emery crime scene. A forensic scientist is working on fibers taken from the site, but so far, we don't have anything."

"Well, at least your unit has identified the McGregor murderer. Now all you have to do is catch him. Something tells me he fled upstate, where I'd been looking for him last month, and then came back to where it's easier to hide— New York City."

"Yeah. Maybe," Vivienne said wryly. "New York isn't that big a city. All we'll have to do is eliminate a couple hundred thousand men Randall Gage's age and description and we'll have him. Easy-peasy. Oh, and I *am* coming with you to interview Mrs. Potter, so you may as well head straight over there."

He glanced at her. "Stubborn."

She laughed. "I'm the stubborn one?" She shook her head and even Caleb had to smile.

# FOURTEEN

Caleb drove to the Potter apartment and flashed his badge to the patrolman standing guard on the sidewalk. "We'll be inside for about a half hour."

"My relief is due any minute," the young officer said. "I'll wait and tell him you're in there."

Nodding, Caleb shepherded Vivienne and Hank ahead of him. "Potters are on the third floor. Does Hank do elevators?"

"If you mean is he scared of them, no. If you're asking does he push the call button himself, no again."

He smiled. "A lack in his training, obviously. I was expecting him to choose the right floor, too."

"He could if I taught him to. It's scary how intelligent our dogs are, especially my Hank."

"Is he the first K-9 you've worked with?" Caleb asked as they boarded and started up.

"Yes. I'm really going to miss him when he ages out of the program. When he does, I'll adopt him. The majority of police dogs are adopted by their handlers." She smiled at Hank. "Then he can spend his old age napping on a soft blanket and vegging out."

"Sounds good to me."

"Are you planning on that for your retirement?"

The elevator doors slid open. Caleb led the way out so he could check the hallway. "You know how it is in our business. Long-range plans are daydreams."

"Right." She was watching Hank sniff the floor. "They know we're coming, don't they?" she asked as they headed down the hall.

"Your boss spoke with Mrs. Potter yesterday and let her know an FBI agent and the K-9 officer who got Jake back would be by to interview her."

He knocked on the door. Noises from inside were muted, mostly covered by the traffic in the street and sounds from nearby apartments.

"Mrs. Potter," Caleb called. "My name is Caleb Black. I'm with the FBI." He held up his badge wallet in front of the peephole on the door.

"And Vivienne Armstrong with the Brooklyn K-9 Unit," she added. "I have my working dog with me."

Stirring behind the apartment door was followed by a high-pitched order. "Stand in front of the peephole and back up. Never mind the badges. Those can be faked. I want to see your faces and the dog."

Seconds after they complied, locks clicked and the door was opened. "Sorry. I wanted to be sure."

"Perfectly understandable," Caleb said. "I'm Agent Black, FBI. You already know Officer Armstrong and Hank."

Tears filled the mother's eyes. She reached for Vivienne's free hand. "Yes. Thank you again. I owe you so, so much. Please, come in and sit down. Can I get you something to drink? Coffee? Tea?" Her hands were fluttering like a bird with a broken wing.

Vivienne led the way as Caleb assessed the small apartment. It was neat, though cluttered. A plastic laundry basket filled with child's toys sat in the center of a worn rug.

"Your son isn't here?" Caleb asked.

"He's still asleep. Last night he was so restless since…well, you know, that I let him nap whenever he would. I can wake him if you want."

"Maybe before we leave so he can hug my dog," Vivienne said. "It's you we came to see." She smiled. "Please, sit down."

Caleb had never seen Vivienne working with a victim before. He was impressed. And, since the nervous woman seemed to take to another female better than to him, he backed off and let her continue while he took notes.

"I told the police all I know," Susanna said, perching on the edge of a chair while keeping an eye on the interior hallway.

"We read your statement, Susanna. May I call you Susanna?"

"Of course."

"Good. I'm Vivienne and this is Hank." She smiled and stroked her K-9's head as he lay at her feet. "There have been some new developments since your ordeal on the promenade and we need to ask you a few questions."

The fluttery hands clasped together. "I'll help if I can. I want that awful person behind bars."

"I'm certain the kidnapper was a woman. The police report notes that Jake said 'a lady took him.'"

Susanna nodded. "Right. I never saw her."

Caleb wanted to jump in but refrained, watching Vivienne's composure and marveling at how calm she seemed. If he hadn't known how important this interview was to her he'd have thought she didn't have a worry in the world.

"When I brought him back to you and officers were questioning the two of you, Jake said he didn't recognize her. Has he said otherwise since?"

She shook her head. "No. He kept saying 'Stranger danger' so he made it crystal clear he'd never seen her before."

"How about you?" Vivienne asked, leaning forward slightly, elbows on her knees. "Do you think you may have passed somebody wearing a gray hoodie and walking shorts before you stopped to look at the boats in the river?"

Tears glistened. "I don't know. I've been wracking my brain ever since it happened. So many people dress that way so I'm sure I did, but we hardly ever look at faces, do we? I mean, the city is full of them but they kind of all blur together."

"Unless we have a good reason to notice. Now, you do. How about since? Have you seen anybody like that hanging around?"

*"Here?"* She jumped to her feet and began to pace. "What's going on? Do you think she'll come back for my baby?"

Caleb thought he was going to have to intervene but Vivienne reached out. "I didn't mean to make you worry. A patrol officer will be stationed outside until she's caught—you already know that, so that has to give you some

peace of mind. And we're working very hard to figure out who she is." Susanna seemed to calm and she sat back down. Vivienne smiled gently. "We just have a few more questions. I promise. Agent Black has a sketch for you to look at."

Pulling a piece of white paper from his coat pocket, he unfolded it and passed it to the fearful mother. "How about this? Have you noticed anybody who looks like her?"

Susanna's hands were shaking. She dashed away stray tears then accepted the computer-generated image. Her brow furrowed.

"Does she look familiar?" Caleb prodded.

"I'm not sure. I'd like to say no but there's something about her that *does* seem familiar. A photograph would be better."

Vivienne's raised hand stopped him from commenting. He sat back and waited. It seemed as if the ensuing minute took thirty to pass. Finally, she said, "Why don't you just start talking? Say anything that pops into your head, even if it seems silly."

"Well…while looking at that picture, I keep thinking of shopping. Fresh produce, maybe. It's almost like I smell ripe cantaloupes. That can't be right. There were no fruit stands by the river."

"No, but you may have subconsciously provided a clue."

"How?"

Caleb finally took over. "Because we strongly suspect that the abduction was not spur-of-the-moment. We think it was planned and carried out after observing you and your son for some time, meaning the perpetrator is likely someone from this neighborhood."

"What?" She was on her feet again. "Why?"

"Because of what's been happening to Officer Armstrong, to Vivienne. There have been specific threats." Experience told him to hold back the more violent details. "Whoever was responsible for taking Jake has zeroed in on her and her K-9 for foiling the abduction. If the kidnapping had been random, the perpetrator should have moved on to a different child, maybe even a different borough. Right now we're concentrating our efforts in Brooklyn, specifically near the promenade."

Speechless, Susanna Potter sank into a chair, acting as if her legs would no longer support her.

"In your previous interview you stated that you took Jake there nearly every morning. Is that correct?"

"Yes. It's such a nice place to get some air."

"Have you been there since?" She knew the answer but wanted to make certain.

"I haven't left this apartment. I'm afraid to."

Rising to move closer, Vivienne commanded Hank to stay and crouched in front of the frightened mother, gently touching her forearm. "We want to suggest that you leave the city for a short time. Is there anywhere you can go? A friend you can stay with, maybe?"

"Preferably not close family," Caleb added. "If you've been targeted the kidnapper may have learned a little about your relatives. It's not as likely, but it is possible."

"Jake's godmother lives in Idaho," Susanna said softly. "We went to college together. I can call her and ask."

"We'll supply a new phone in case your old one has been compromised. You'll need to write down any pertinent information so we can get in touch with you once this case is solved."

Vivienne had remained at Susanna's feet. Now, she straightened and pulled up the fearful woman beside her. "I'll help you pack while Agent Black takes care of the details. Give us your friend's name and address so he can book a flight." A hand signal brought Hank to her side. "Let's go surprise Jake with a visit from

his favorite K-9 and let them get reacquainted while we pack."

*Smooth*, Caleb thought. Calmly and successfully done with no hair-pulling or wailing. The K-9 cop was good at her job.

Meaning this was exactly where she belonged, he concluded. There was no way he'd be able to talk her into going into another line of work for her own safety, nor would he try.

For a reason he was nowhere near ready to accept, that conclusion hurt.

Little Jake wasn't asleep. The moment he spotted his furry rescuer he jumped out of bed and threw his arms around the K-9's neck. "I love puppies!"

"Hank loves you, too, honey, but you need to remember that not all dogs are this friendly," Vivienne warned.

Susanna reaffirmed it. "That's right, baby. There are mean doggies, too. You need to ask Mommy before you try to hug them."

His shoulders sagged and he lowered his arms. "Sorry."

Vivienne had one hand on Hank's silky fur to help keep him from getting too excited while he was harnessed to work. "It's okay this time. Just keep him company more qui-

etly. See his vest? That means he's on the job and shouldn't be playing."

Wide, innocent blue eyes looked up at her. "Take it off."

"I can't do that right now," Vivienne said. "You and your mom are going to take a trip. Why don't you go pick out a couple of toys to take with you? Ones that will fit into a suitcase, okay?" Seeing him shy away and retreat to his bed, she smiled. "It's okay. Hank and I will go with you to the airport. We'll keep you safe. I promise."

"I don't wanna go."

"You and your mother will get to ride on a big airplane. It'll be fun. You'll see."

As he pulled the cover over his head, she heard a muffled "No."

There were tears in Susanna's eyes. "I can't make him go out when he's so scared."

"You need to take care of him the best way possible and if that means leaving the city, you will. You must."

"Why? Just because you say there were threats? Because you and the FBI agent have made up your minds we're in danger? I don't think so."

Vivienne told Hank to stay. "Let's leave your little boy where he is and go to your room."

"I'm not packing a bag because I'm not leaving."

"Fine. We still need to talk privately. Please?" Leading the way into the hall, Vivienne eased the door to the boy's room closed, then did the same to the room she and Susanna entered.

The slightly younger woman struck a pose, hands fisted on her hips. "I'm not changing my mind."

"That's your prerogative. I was hoping I wouldn't have to tell you what's happened to me, but I can see no alternative."

The tilt of Susanna's head and the dubious-looking arch of her eyebrows affirmed Vivienne's decision to speak out. "Since Hank tracked down your son and his kidnapper from the promenade, I've been shot at. And stalked."

"No!"

"Yes. There has been a threatening phone call made to the station, too." She paused, then added the most frightening event. "A bomb was left outside the door to my apartment. I was staying in an FBI safe house, but it was compromised."

Susanna bit her lip.

"That doesn't matter. What does is that I'm a sworn, armed police officer and I've had to move my residence…temporarily. You're a ci-

vilian who has to rely on outside sources of protection that may or may not be available when you need them."

The other woman sank onto the edge of her bed and doubled over, head in her hands. "This is a nightmare."

"I won't argue that. What you need to remember is that your little boy is counting on you to do what's best for him. In my opinion, the best thing is to leave here, where you're known, and go someplace new. If money is a problem there are programs that will help out. You might even qualify for temporary relocation if…" Vivienne had an idea. "I'll be right back."

Caleb rose when she reentered the living room. "Is she ready to go?"

"Not quite." She held out a hand. "Give me that printout of the face."

The instant he produced it she snatched it from him and whirled. Susanna had gone to her son's room and was rocking him while she wept silently.

Vivienne didn't hesitate. "Jake. Remember the bad stranger who grabbed you?"

Susanna pulled him closer, shielding his face. "Get away. You're scaring him."

"No. This is necessary. Please. Let him look at this picture." She crouched next to the bed

and drew her K-9 into the group. "My dog isn't scared to look. See?"

One big blue eye peeked from behind Susanna's shoulder.

"It's just a piece of paper with a drawing on it. All you need to do is look at it and tell me if this is the bad lady."

Wiggling, he turned slightly in his mother's arms.

Vivienne smoothed the folds in the paper and held it up for him. One look and terror filled his features. She didn't need verbal confirmation although she got it, anyway, when the boy screeched and threw both arms around his mother's neck.

That poor boy. If leaving filled him with terror, which Vivienne just added to, maybe staying in the apartment would be okay for a little while. She and Caleb would just have to find the kidnapper—and Vivienne's stalker—fast. "Okay. I'm convinced that staying might be in Jake's best interest," Vivienne said. "Stay put. I'll go tell Agent Black."

"Wait!" Susanna said with a shudder. "Tell him to get the tickets. I'll call my boss and ask for some time off. We're leaving."

# FIFTEEN

Caleb was still working with law enforcement to arrange a relocation for a safe house for him and Vivienne, using his office as liaison, when they reached the airport. JFK was a main hub so there was plenty of traffic and good opportunities to lose themselves in the crowds, particularly in Terminal 8.

He turned to Vivienne. "You stand out like a beacon. You and the dog should stay with my SUV. We'll use the daily parking to unload baggage and I'll escort our guests to their gate. That way I'll know exactly where you are."

"Excuse me?"

"Sorry. I'll rephrase. Officer Armstrong, since your uniform and K-9 will make you particularly visible to one and all, would you please stay with my car? I would be most grateful and it is best for my other passengers if they don't attract attention while boarding."

"Well, since you put it that way…"

"Good."

Caleb handled Mrs. Potter's wheeled suit-case while she carried her toddler. Traffic was thick. Their only obstacles were taxis that were permitted to unload directly in front of the ter-minal and were jockeying for curb space.

On full alert, he took Susanna Potter's arm to hurry her safely past. "Once you're through TSA you'll be going on alone," Caleb said.

"No!"

"You'll be fine at that point." He kept walk-ing. "I don't want to call attention to my FBI status by flashing a badge and insisting I wait with you at the gate. My office has stationed extra uniformed transit cops near your depar-ture point so feel free to ask any of them for assistance if you feel you need it."

"What about when we land?"

"You'll be met by local police and escorted to your friend's home. From there on it's up to you to be vigilant. Little Jake can ID his kid-napper so it's really imperative to keep him safe and secluded."

"You don't think that awful woman would try to follow us, do you?"

"No, I really don't. Jake will be safe now." He set her bag on the TSA conveyor belt and handed her the ticket folder. "Boarding pass

is in there. Get out your driver's license and you're good to go."

Monitoring her travels through the security system, he stayed on edge until the call for boarding, when she passed through the final checkpoint. Nobody without a valid ticket could catch up to her now, which is why his next stop was the airline ticket counter, where he inquired about available seating, just in case.

"I'm sorry, sir. That flight is fully booked. I can get you a seat for this afternoon."

"Everybody has checked in already?"

"Yes, sir."

"No chance of last-minute openings?"

"Sorry. No."

"Okay. Never mind. I'll pass this time."

Leaving the counter attendant looking puzzled, Caleb turned and strode toward the exit. The sooner he rejoined Vivienne, the happier he'd be.

He was jogging by the time he turned the last corner and spied his vehicle. He'd purposely parked with the hood and front bumper sticking out beyond others in the row, making it easy to spot from a distance.

Arriving at the driver's door, he grabbed the handle and jerked. Locked. Tinted windows kept him from seeing inside clearly. He cupped

his hands around his eyes and peered through, expecting either the uniformed officer or the dog or both.

Not only was Vivienne missing, but her K-9 was, too!

Vivienne had meant to keep her promise to Caleb. And she would have if she hadn't thought she'd spotted the very woman who had become her nemesis.

The sun was high, making it hard to see details clearly, so she opted for taking a couple of photos with her phone. Everything about this person was screaming that she was the right one. So now what? If she failed to follow her, to see where she went and who she might be with, she'd be giving up a chance to put an end to the harassment. And to the life-threatening attacks.

The woman didn't come closer, as Vivienne had hoped. Instead, she was wandering around the lot as if she'd forgotten where she'd parked. Maybe she wasn't who Vivienne had thought she was after all. The only way to find out was to follow her.

Slipping from the SUV with Hank leashed at her side, Vivienne had ventured a short way from Caleb's vehicle. Never once did she make eye contact with her quarry, but after a few

minutes she did conclude that the woman's movements appeared more furtive than before. Not only that, but she and her dog were also getting farther and farther from the FBI car.

Vivienne was staring at the computer-generated images stored on her cell phone when it vibrated. *Caleb.* If their witness was safely in the air it would be a relief.

The booming voice that answered her pleasant "hello" was so loud she held the phone away.

"Where are you?" he demanded.

"Not far. I think the kidnapper may be here," Vivienne said. "I tried to get a good picture, but she was looking the other way, so I—"

"Tell me you didn't go after her."

"Calm down. I'm an armed law-enforcement officer, remember? I think Hank may be able to track her scent if I can show him which one I want him to follow."

"No!"

"Yes. You're blowing this way out of proportion." Her breathing was rapid as she swiveled to reassess her surroundings. "And now you've made me lose sight of her."

"Direction?"

"Why?"

"North, south, east or west? I'm coming. You need backup."

"Don't." Vivienne huffed, knowing he was right. "Okay, I'll turn back. The heat is starting to bother Hank, and we can cover the parking lot faster in your SUV. Be right there."

Relying on her sense of direction, and on Hank, she ended the phone conversation and made her way toward Caleb as quickly as possible, cutting across lanes and slipping between parked vehicles until she could finally see him. His tie was loosened and hanging lopsided, his face was flushed and his hair looked as if he'd been repeatedly running his fingers through it. Poor guy. He looked nearly frantic. And for no reason. She was fine.

Vivienne stepped into view and waved her arm overhead, intending to put his mind at ease first, then chastise him later when he'd settled down. It was one thing to show concern for a partner in the field and quite another to become unnecessarily distressed.

Caleb turned back to the black SUV without any more acknowledgment of her than a nod, calling over his shoulder.

She started down a row of cars, keeping Hank on a loose lead. Her mind was centered on Caleb, which bothered her because she knew the distraction was counterproductive. What she… What they both should be thinking about was doing their jobs, starting with

the possibility that she actually had spotted her elusive stalker.

If she got another opportunity, she'd try to put her K-9 on the trail, as she should have done to start with, she concluded, as upset with herself as she was with Caleb. Even without a scent object Hank might have been able to sort out the right odor and track it, since the sighting of the wandering woman was so fresh.

Caleb paused at the driver's door of his SUV with his hand on the lock, then looked up. Centered on her. His jaw slackened. Eyes widened. "Vivienne! Look out!"

She heard a roar behind her, saw Caleb draw his gun and start to move. Pivoting, she froze for a split second. A speeding car was bearing down on her. Hank! She had to save Hank above all.

Her arms waved, giving the dog direction as she dropped the end of the leash. "Go! Go!"

Spinning on his haunches, the border collie did exactly as ordered. He took off running— away from her.

Had she not taken that precaution she would have had more time to guard her own body. By the time she looked back to see where the speeding car was, it was nearly upon her.

Caleb had stepped dead center into the traffic lane between rows of parked cars and assumed

a shooter's stance, feet apart, hands together on his Glock, arms extended. "Stop. FBI!"

The tan car kept coming. Faster and faster. Seconds elapsed in slow motion, giving Vivienne the illusion of having time to seek safety. She actually had no chance to think, let alone plan. If she didn't move she was going to be badly hurt. Or worse. Leaping to the side between a parked car and a cement-filled end post, she smashed into the narrow yellow marker column, bounced off and fell, stunned.

The older model tan car zigzagged past and on down the aisle, avoiding Caleb and taking the turn at the end with a screech of slipping tires. Metal crunched as the car caromed off the rear bumper of a parked pickup truck.

Vivienne briefly assessed her physical condition before moving. Her world was off-kilter. Shimmering. Spinning. But she was alive. And except for a sore knee and a badly bruised ego, she was unhurt. Given the circumstances, that was a win in her book. One that deserved thanks.

Waiting for her equilibrium to return, she closed her eyes and prayed, "Thank You, Lord. Again."

# SIXTEEN

Caleb thought his heart had literally stopped beating. Vivienne was down. Had she been hit? Injured? He could see a little movement, but she wasn't getting up.

He was at her side in mere seconds and reached for her past Hank, who had returned and was licking her cheeks. "Are you okay?" Caleb shouted. "Did they get you? Sideswipe you? Talk to me!"

"I'm okay. A little banged up. A concrete post attacked me after the car missed."

Feeling her firm grip on his hands helped. So did pulling her to her feet, so he could look directly into her eyes. "You really are okay?"

"Yes."

Caleb didn't break eye contact and, thankfully, neither did she. There was an unspoken connection between them that reached into his heart. He couldn't keep from gazing into the bottomless depths of her eyes until he

saw them begin to grow misty. That was more than enough incentive to pull her fully into an embrace. As he did, he felt her slip her arms around his waist.

He remained vigilant, continuing to watch for threats, while Vivienne leaned against him as if they had always been this close. Although he feared he might be imagining the sincerity of her response to his hug, he chose to prolong it, anyway. It had been a long, long time since he'd felt even a whisper of connection to another person and he was reluctant to let her go.

Vivienne's cheek rested against his chest. He felt her shudder, then finally start to lean away. Instinct urged him to grasp her tightly, but common sense convinced him to relax his hold. When she looked up at him there was something different in her gaze, a quality that surpassed appreciation or mere friendship. Best of all, it bore no resemblance to the pity he had noticed from others. Vivienne wasn't feeling sorry for his loneliness, she was somehow erasing the pain a little at a time.

That thought brought him up short. Having grieved and held on to his anger for seven years, this sense of belonging was frightening.

To Caleb's relief, Vivienne began to smile. "Whew! That was a close one."

"Yeah." He swallowed past a lump in his throat. "Too close."

She glanced down at the K-9 happily spinning in circles at their feet. "At least Hank is okay. Did you get a license number?"

Caleb shook his head. "No, the angle of the sun made it hard to see anything straight on. Did you?"

"Uh-uh. I did see something odd, though." Still holding her hands, he felt her fingers tighten on his as her eyes widened. "It was like I was seeing double."

"Are you now?" He grasped her shoulders and held her still, facing him. "If your vision's been affected, you'll need to go to ER to be checked out."

"No, no. My eyes are fine. It was before the car passed. There were two people in the front seat."

"Men or women?"

"Women. Both of them."

She was beginning to tremble, so he looped one arm around her shoulders to guide her back to his car. "Did you get a good look?"

"Good enough. The passenger was the spitting image of my kidnapper sketch." Caleb started to reach for his phone.

"Wait," she said abruptly, "there's more."

He could tell she'd been shocked and as-

sumed she was reacting to the near miss until she said, "The second person. The driver. She looked enough like our suspect to be her sister or daughter. We were right about there being two of them. Maybe they were both there when I was shot at the first time. It would explain a lot."

That deduction didn't change anything for Caleb other than to increase his vigilance. He beeped his key to unlock the SUV, helped her into the passenger seat and checked her condition once again while Hank hopped the center console and made himself at home in the second seat. "Your pupils are equal and normal."

"That's a plus," she said, still smiling.

Before shutting her door he asked, "Where to? The hospital or our new safe house? My boss arranged it. Not far from the old one but even more private."

"The station. I want to talk to my boss while everything is fresh in my mind."

"You can do that from the house. I'll set up a video-conferencing call." Caleb's jaw clenched. He could tell she was about to shoot down his idea and countermand his orders, such as they were. Insisting he was right was going to get him nowhere. Fast.

After shutting the passenger door, he strode to the other side and slid behind the wheel.

Then he used his radio to report the attack at the airport.

"Tan with New York plates," he said. "Two female passengers in the front seats. We'll need to check the video from the parking-lot cameras for thirty minutes on either side of the present time. If we don't see the right car on that footage, pull traffic cams for the off-ramps from Van Wyck and surface roads leading to Terminal Eight."

"What's your twenty?" Dispatch asked.

"We're still at the airport. I'll stop at Security and inform them of the attack, although I doubt they'll be too concerned since nobody was hurt. And I'll leave my card on the parked truck that the fleeing suspects bumped in case they want to report a scratched bumper."

"Will you be requesting a crime scene team?"

Caleb paused then said, "No. I don't think they left anything behind from the collision, but I will go check more closely before we bother to bring in techs."

"Copy. Out."

Backing out, Caleb cruised slowly past the large pickup truck that had been hit, carefully scanning the pavement while Vivienne leaned out her window and did the same. "Do you see

anything?" he asked. "Glass or chrome? Paint left behind. Anything?"

"Nope," she replied. "I guess they weren't traveling as fast as it seemed when they almost mowed me down."

"Fast enough to have flattened you," Caleb stressed. "You do know that, don't you?"

"Yes. I guess there's not going to be any place where I'm safe until we catch them."

"I'm relieved to hear you say that."

"I've *always* been cautious," Vivienne argued. "I don't like having to take that to extremes."

"You know what they say." Caleb paused for emphasis. "Tough."

"Yeah. I've been told that before."

He caught a glimpse of her hand reaching toward him then retreating and he wanted desperately to comfort her more. When he'd seen her in mortal danger his whole being had responded. That had been a more emotional response than was called for, he knew, yet if he'd had to do it again he knew he'd embrace her. Gladly.

When he'd seen that near miss he'd aged a hundred years! Caleb swallowed past a cottony throat. Milliseconds had separated Vivienne from grave bodily injury. She could easily have been killed while he stood there, trying to de-

cide if it was safe to discharge his weapon in such a well-used area.

It wasn't safe so he'd let the car pass. Seen Vivienne on the ground. And thought for a heart-wrenching moment that he'd just watched someone else he cared about die.

Processing all that information brought a simple conclusion. Their relationship had crossed the threshold from platonic to something approaching romantic, and he couldn't deny it. Caleb slowed and pulled to the curb, before they reached the security offices. He undid his seat belt so he could swivel to face her.

Although not a word passed between them, she did the same. He once again opened his arms. And Vivienne leaned into his embrace as naturally as if they had done it hundreds of times before.

The silent kisses he placed on her hair went unnoticed, he hoped. It was all he could do to keep from weeping in gratitude for her survival. He would never allow himself to show that much emotion, of course.

So he held her. Stroked her back gently and felt her arms slide around past his shoulder holster. There was nothing he could say, nothing he could tell her, that would explain how he felt. Truth to tell, he wasn't all that sure

himself. Sensible thoughts and conclusions no longer matched his innermost feelings and the conflict was jarring.

His whole world was tilted on its axis. Nothing made sense anymore, least of all what he was doing in this very moment. Worse, he yearned to kiss her properly. What was wrong with him? He'd shunned romance for seven long years, yet it had taken only two days to change that comfortable outlook and leave him wondering if he'd lost his mind. This woman craved the one thing he could never give again. A family. Children.

From his broken heart came a plea that was also new. He called out to God. *Please, please, help me just walk away when all this is over.*

Caleb started to lean back, to relax his embrace, and she did the same. Her expressive eyes glistened. Her soft lips trembled. She wanted him to kiss her—he knew she did.

He wasn't going to give in no matter how much he wanted to.

A wet tongue slurped the side of his face. Rapid panting sent K-9 breath right after it. The shock was more than adequate to break Caleb's train of thought.

Apparently, it was enough for Vivienne, too, because she giggled and moved away, blush-

ing. "I forgot to mention," she said between chuckles, "Hank gets jealous sometimes."

Caleb was pretty sure his prayers had just been answered although not in the manner he'd imagined they would be. He still wanted to kiss Vivienne. He still wanted to hug her. But, fortunately, they had a four-legged chaperone along for the ride, one who would be with her 24/7.

Grinning, he reached back to ruffle Hank's ears, grinned and said, "Thanks, buddy. I owe you one."

Vivienne fought to catch her breath. To understand what had just happened and maybe make a little sense of it. She was more than confused. She was astounded. And shocked. And way, way too happy about what Caleb had done.

As he started the engine and pulled back into traffic, she worked to show convincing nonchalance. She needed to pretend that she hugged all her partners the way she'd hugged Caleb.

An amusing thought intruded. She did hug the four-legged ones. That hardly counted, did it? People—men in particular—had always seemed standoffish compared to the way her heart responded to them. And in those cases

she'd known better than to be too demonstrative. That was another good thing about little kids. They were almost always ready to accept and return affection without asking questions or overanalyzing.

*Say something. Anything,* she thought, wishing at first that Caleb could read her mind, then taking it back when she realized what kind of personal thoughts he would be privy to. If she wasn't so rattled this situation would actually be funny. Perhaps the best way to deal with her feelings was to make jokes about them.

"I hope I evaded that speeding car gracefully," she told Caleb. "I wouldn't want to look awkward on the video footage."

"*That's* what you're worried about?"

She raised the hand closest to him. "I was just kidding. I will be interested in seeing if it came as close as it felt."

"It wasn't far off." His hands were fisted on the wheel.

"Sorry if I scared you. I scared myself, too."

"You have to stop acting as though you have a death wish, okay? You're giving me gray hair."

Eyeing his dark blond, short cut, she laughed. "I don't see one gray hair."

"All my hair was brown last week," Caleb teased. "Then I came to Brooklyn and met you."

"Yeah, yeah." Sobering slightly, she continued to smile. "I really do love my job, you know."

"I get it. I wish I'd been on the promenade sooner and could have watched you and your K-9 track the boy."

"He really was something," Vivienne said with tenderness. She turned enough to reach back and pet Hank. He immediately responded, wagging his tail, licking her fingertips and panting gaily. "Yes. Good boy," she cooed.

Acting delighted, the border collie pranced on the leading edge of the seat, then lunged to bestow another kiss on Caleb's right ear and cheek.

"Thanks, Hank. But maybe not when I'm driving."

"What, you don't like kisses on the road?" Vivienne dissolved into giggles, attributing her reaction to being uptight.

Caleb arched an eyebrow and gave her a sidelong glance. "Not the dog kind."

If she had been braver and hadn't still been trying to figure out how she felt about a man she hardly knew, she might have picked up on his comment and made a witty remark.

Thinking about how close she and Caleb had come to perhaps actually kissing, her mind

went blank. If someone had demanded she quote her name and badge number right now, she doubted she could have done it.

Worse, they had arrived at the security booth for that section of the parking lot and he was stopping. Time to stop thinking about kissing.

That conclusion made her blush. It was not going to be easy.

# SEVENTEEN

Caleb had been right about the reaction he'd get when he reported the incident, and Vivienne told him so. Cars sped in the airport parking lots and its tiered structure all the time so minor fender-benders were part of a guard's day. Nevertheless, she felt better after they had alerted the security staff.

"We'll make a full report once we get back to your station," Caleb told her. "Brooklyn police can formally request the license number from airport-security cameras, which will probably also give us an ID of the driver. Now that we know there are two women involved it should make the investigation easier. Age won't play as big a part and if we can spot one, she should lead us to the other."

"What do you think? Are they sisters or mother and daughter?"

"Could be either. Without observing the family dynamics between them it's hard to say.

If it's mother and daughter, chances are the mother is in charge. With sisters it will depend on birth order and strengths of personality."

"The more I picture their faces, the more I think they're mother and daughter. But that still doesn't explain why they abducted the Potter boy or why they're so mad at me for stopping them."

"Time will tell. Have patience," Caleb said.

"I'm just nervous. I can't seem to shake the idea that I'm being watched. Know what I mean? It's like, wherever I go, there's somebody out to get me. I can't go home, I can't ride with you to the airport. I can't even safely walk between the station and training facility. How am I going to do my job?"

"Very carefully," he drawled.

Vivienne had to study his face for a second before she was sure he was trying to make a joke to lighten her mood. "Good idea, but it doesn't do much to help my nerves. I feel like I'm climbing the walls."

"Of the Empire State Building?"

"No, smarty. That was too hard to do the first time I tried."

Caleb laughed. "Sounds like something you might do."

She noticed him sobering as he checked traf-

fic behind them on the expressway. "Do you see somebody following us?"

"I don't think so. It's pretty hard to drive and keep a close watch, though."

She looked in her side mirror. No sign of a tan car. Then she turned around as best she could with the seat belt on to check out the back windshield. She didn't see the car.

She saw him cast a quick glance in his side mirror, then jerk his head toward her. "Possible trouble."

"Did you see the tan car that tried to run over me?"

"I think so. There's only one way to tell for sure. Tell Hank to get down on the floor so he doesn't slide around. We're about to go for a wild ride."

Caleb didn't begin evasive tactics until he was certain his passengers were safe and secure. He pressed on the accelerator and whipped the wheel, passing several cars at once as he changed lanes, then pulled back into the lane he'd been in before.

That kind of abrupt lane change wasn't too rare in city traffic and it gave him the perfect chance to watch the car he suspected. When it followed his pattern he made a second quick maneuver, using a box truck as a foil and dart-

ing in front of it. The driver honked and shook his fist.

Vivienne was watching via the side mirror and noticed the angry truck driver. "That guy's upset."

"Can't be helped. Defensive driving is just part of the job. It's other people's reactions I can't control."

"Right. We don't want to scare them enough to cause an accident."

"Exactly." At least she wasn't arguing with him. That was a plus. So was the box truck because it was riding his bumper so closely no other cars could squeeze in.

"Back two car lengths and to my left, in the fast lane," Caleb said, realizing he was nearly shouting. "Can you tell if that's them?"

She swiveled as far as the tight belt would allow, then slipped her right shoulder free to turn farther. "Looks like it. I can't be absolutely positive, but I think so."

"Okay. Call your station and tell them we think we're being followed by the same car that almost ran you down at the airport."

As she made the call, he assessed traffic, hoping to be able to slip into the far right lane, slow down enough to drop back, then fall in behind the tan car to turn the tables on the occupants. That would help them see the license

plate and positively match it when they got the closed-circuit pictures from airport parking.

Traffic was both a help and a hindrance. He didn't dare signal his intent to change lanes when the tan car was close enough to observe him. He also didn't want to cause a wreck or involve innocent civilians.

Several failed attempts made him decide to change tactics. He radioed an updated call for backup on the police frequency and was told response would be delayed so he went to plan B.

"I'm going to try to pull off at an exit while our friends in the other car are still cut off by the truck. Hang on."

"That's too risky," Vivienne countered.

"Only if the drivers I need to pass are daydreaming or talking on cell phones. I'm afraid if we stay here they'll eventually catch up to us and either take a shot at you or try to ram us. Either way they're liable to cause a terrible pileup. We can't take that chance."

"I don't like any of our choices."

"Join the club. Just keep a lookout. You won't be able to see if they're behind us until I hit the off-ramp," Caleb said loudly. "Watch in that outside mirror and hang on. If they try to follow us we'll advise our backup that the situation has worsened."

"I wouldn't dream of letting go," Vivienne

yelled back. She cast a brief glance over her left shoulder, apparently checking on her K-9 because she added, "Stay!"

Caleb saw his chance coming up. Almost there. Almost in the clear.

At the last possible second, he veered to the right, tires bumping over a row of raised warning dots on the pavement. "Made it!"

The box truck crossed behind the SUV and blocked his view. Cars ahead were slowing. If he'd been successful in eluding their trackers, he'd bought them time. If not, he'd better be ready for a possible assault on foot.

Beside him, Vivienne was peering into the mirror. "I can't tell!" She swiveled as far as the seat belt would allow. "I don't think they made it off when we did."

"I don't see their car," Caleb said. His palms drummed against the steering wheel as if that would make the cars ahead clear the street. "Come on, come on, come on."

"Push your button to change the signal so we get through the intersections faster," she ordered.

"That's a fire-department, patrol-officer, ambulance gadget," Caleb countered. "I don't have one."

"Super. So drive on the shoulder."

"Only if I have to," he said. "Just keep

watching. If you see anybody approaching on foot, let me know."

Her eyes were rolling, her eyebrows arching when she turned to him. "Wow. Like, you think I wouldn't mention it?"

"Okay, okay. I get so focused on keeping you safe that sometimes I forget you're a cop." The moment the words left his mouth he knew he was in trouble.

Vivienne made a face at him. "You sometimes forget I'm a cop? Listen Mr. FBI Agent, having a K-9 partner makes me a bigger and better threat than you and your badge together. And don't you forget it."

"I really didn't mean that the way it came out," Caleb said. "I apologize. I know you're a cop—and a good one."

When she didn't respond he added, "Please? Forgive me?"

"I'll think about it. If the dog says you're still okay I won't hold that part of the ridiculous statement against you."

"Thanks. I think."

Traffic slowly moved ahead and Caleb was able to enter a side street. "Still no signs of our tail," he reported, starting to relax. "You can let Hank up off the floor now."

"You just want to see if he still likes you."

Caleb had to smile in spite of their recent

close call and misunderstanding. "Anything that makes you forgive me for coming across like I don't appreciate your skill and training is fine with me," he said. "I do respect you as a fellow officer. It's just…" He'd been going to tell her how attractive she was and just how strongly his instincts insisted he must protect her. That admission would have made things worse, of course, so instead he said, "It's the dog. There's something warm and fuzzy about your working dog that I don't see in German shepherds or Rotties or those other imposing breeds. Hank looks too lovable."

To his relief, Vivienne nodded. "I get it. I do. But don't sell him short. He may be the happiest-looking K-9 in my unit, but he's all business when he's put on a trail. You'll see. I'm really proud of the work he does."

"So I'm forgiven?"

The lopsided smile she gave him was almost convincing. Then she gave Hank a hand signal and he jumped back onto the seat behind them.

Caleb watched in the mirror. The dog never took his eyes off her until she said, "Release," and then he morphed into a friendly backyard pet.

The tongue was quick but Caleb was quicker. His hand blocked the slurp headed for his ear. He chuckled. "Convinced?"

Although Vivienne was laughing, he could tell part of it was due to lingering nervousness. "Yes. You passed the pup test. Anybody who is okayed by my dog is okay in my book."

"And anybody he doesn't like?"

"Deserves watching," she said as her smile grew and evened. "His instincts have never failed me."

"Does he have to pass judgment on the guys you pick from the dating app you were telling Penny about? I can't believe a woman like you needs to find dates that way."

She huffed. "It's the gun and badge. You might sometimes forget I'm a cop, but the rest of the world doesn't."

"Hey, I thought I was forgiven for sounding like a jerk."

"You are."

Despite the thick traffic he kept watching for Vivienne's nemesis. "Keep checking behind us and at cross streets. Even if they didn't get off the expressway when we did they may guess you're headed back to your station and be waiting."

"You really think it was them following us, don't you?"

Caleb nodded. "Yes. I do. And I don't expect them to give up easily, especially now that we know two are working together. One person

might get discouraged. Two can bolster each other and will be far more likely to continue."

"That's what I hate about hanging out with truthful people," Vivienne said, smirking at him. "They tell it like it is and I have to accept it." She snorted derisively. "Thanks."

"You're welcome," Caleb said, meaning every word. If they had to accept a truth they didn't like, why not share the burden with each other?

Sighing, she sank a little lower in her seat. "Sometimes I feel like a lame hamster trying to run on a broken exercise wheel. I make a little progress, then boom."

"Please. I worry enough already. Don't remind me about the bomb."

"Believe it or not, I'd forgotten about that. There's already so much to remember, the threats that didn't part my hair are fading into the background."

"It will be over soon," he promised. "We'll get you out of this mess soon."

She was half-smiling when she glanced over at him and said, "From your lips to God's ears."

Caleb didn't even try to reply.

# EIGHTEEN

The following day and night passed in a blur. Vivienne was glad she had a new safe temporary home but regretted the forced closeness to the enigmatic FBI agent. Most of the time they maneuvered around each other as if avoiding inevitable contact. It was the most awkward tango she'd ever tried to dance and the tension of being stuck in the house together was getting to her.

Caleb had made an appointment to interview little Lucy Emery before submitting the profile he'd written of the killer, or killers, of her parents and the McGregor parents. Randall Gage's DNA matched the sample on the watchband found at the McGregor crime scene, but there was no tie to the Emery murders. She wondered if Caleb was right about his theory that the Emery murderer was a copycat. Vivienne was determined to accompany him when he spoke with the child.

"Lucy's only three," Vivienne argued. "You're a big, scary guy. You'll get better results if Hank and I go with you."

"I'll do fine. Penelope McGregor is going to sit in with me because she has such good rapport with the child. That was the only way Detective Nate Slater and his wife, Willow, would permit Lucy to meet with me." Whenever Vivienne thought of how Lucy's aunt and the detective who'd first investigated the Emery murders had fallen in love and become a family with Lucy, her heart warmed.

"I know I'm not assigned to the murder case. I just think having Hank—and me—in the room will be a good addition."

"I already have Slater and his working dog, Willow, Penelope and maybe her brother, Bradley, and his K-9, for backup, plus me. That should be quite a crowd."

"So one more won't matter."

"Two more. You're a duo, in case you've forgotten."

Vivienne reached down to scratch behind Hank's silky ears. "Never. My partner and I are inseparable. Remember last night on the sofa."

She saw Caleb's cheeks flush. Blonds had the kind of complexion that showed the slightest warming and he fit that mold perfectly,

even if he had let his chin get scruffy while they were out of the public eye.

"How could I forget?" Caleb asked, deadpan. "He snores. At first I thought it was you making all that racket."

Picturing them both falling asleep sitting up on the sofa with Hank lying upside down between them made Vivienne chuckle. "It was funny. I don't even remember what movie we were watching. I couldn't seem to keep my eyes open and the next thing I knew, all three of us were sawing logs."

"Uh-huh. And your dog was lying between us doing his dead-squirrel-in-the-road impression."

Vivienne smiled. "I know what you mean. When he rolls over with all four paws in the air and lets his head hang off the edge of the cushions that's exactly what he looks like."

"I suspect I may miss him when we're done with this assignment," Caleb admitted, sobering.

Vivienne noted that he had not said he would miss her. Well, so what? Just because he'd hugged her a few times didn't mean he was ready for commitment, let alone the kind of life she'd envisioned for herself, and she'd be wise to keep that in mind, regardless.

Analyzing her recently turbulent emotions,

she decided it was time to alter the situation, to ask for relief from the constant togetherness that was obviously counterproductive, particularly with regard to her personal feelings.

She chose to speak her thoughts in a way she hoped he would understand. "It's not your fault but I'm suffocating here at the safe house, Caleb. I need to move, to jog, to exercise my K-9, to go back to work full-time so I can feel useful." She paused for emphasis and pointed to the kitchen. "And I need to stop eating balanced meals instead of easy, uncomplicated PBJs." *Plus, I need an uncomplicated life*, she added silently.

"Not good for you," he argued. "Besides, I thought you liked my cooking."

"That's part of the problem. It's your cooking, not mine. I don't want to be coddled. I want to stand on my own two feet and decide what I do or don't want to eat. Where I want to go. What I want to do all day."

"You're so set in your ways as a single person that you probably scare off any guys who'd give you that big family you say you want."

Thinking he was done, Vivienne opened her mouth to tell him off but he interrupted. "A family isn't a dictatorship, lady, it's a co-op. The best is with two parents who think alike so they present a united front to their kids. They

have to support each other, give and take, not decide on a boss and an underling. Not if they want to be happy. And don't get me started on raising kids or we'll be here all morning."

"Are you done?"

"No, but I'll stop."

"Thank you. So since I'm not sitting in on the interview with Lucy Emery, are you going to drive me to the station with you, or do I have to wait until you're gone and then call a cab?"

"Those are my choices?"

She raised her chin and stood tall. "Yes."

"I'm leaving in thirty minutes," he said. "Be ready."

He didn't know her very well if he thought a time limit would deter her, did he? She could be dressed and out the door in half the time he'd allotted. Getting ready was easy. Forgetting what he'd said to her about families wasn't. She'd hated growing up without her much older brother, assuming the main drawback was loneliness. Now, she was beginning to realize that being raised alone may not have equipped her for caring for the big family she craved. Maybe that was why the good Lord hadn't brought her a husband. She'd certainly tried hard enough to find one on her own.

Vivienne brushed her hair and whisked on a light lip gloss, then strapped on her utility belt

and holster. Hank was so excited he couldn't stand still. Racing in circles, he passed the window several times before sticking his nose behind the heavy drapes and giving a single, high-pitched woof.

Vivienne joined him, pulled back the drape at one side and looked out. Nothing seemed amiss. And Hank's bark hadn't been the kind he used for a warning—it was more joyful and excited. Nevertheless, she carefully scanned the residential street.

The weight of her gun and holster were comforting. So was the thought that Caleb would be with her.

That was another problem with being idle in the safe house. Too much time to think, to imagine, to let her mind paint pretty pictures as well as ugly ones.

Reality was what she craved most. Even if it proved dangerous.

Caleb checked his watch when he saw her coming. He should have known she'd be early. There wasn't a lot of mystery left between them...

"Ready?" Vivienne asked without her usual smile.

"Yes. You?"

She turned a full circle. "Of course. To be

safe, I want a protective vest, and Hank's, too. The extras you got are out in your car."

"They were. I brought them in." He gestured toward the kitchen table. "Help yourself."

"I'll be glad to get my own vest from head-quarters. It fits better."

"You mean, it doesn't say FBI in big white letters, don't you?" he said, getting the smile he was looking for.

"Well, there is that, too."

"Thought so." He, too, donned his own bulletproof vest then started for the side door that led to the garage, expecting her to follow. When she didn't, he looked back. "Coming?"

"Before we go I want to thank you for everything you've done. I know I haven't been the best housemate and I do apologize. This has been difficult for me." *Difficult? Talk about an understatement.*

Jaw firm, shoulders squared, he nodded as he turned away. "Apology accepted and same here."

She nodded. "Good." Vivienne and Hank breezed past him. She opened the side door and let the K-9 precede her.

As she got Hank settled in the SUV and then fastened her seat belt, Caleb slid behind the wheel and pressed the overhead-door re-

mote. As the heavy mechanized door lifted, he started the engine and backed out.

The neighborhood seemed quiet at this time of day. Residents who went to regular nine-to-five jobs had left, children were back in school and anyone who wanted to putter in the yard had been driven inside by the building heat.

He upped the AC in the car. "Cool enough for you?"

"Yes. Thanks. Wearing this vest is like living in a sauna."

"Yeah."

One of the reasons he'd wanted to conduct his interview of little Lucy at the Brooklyn K-9 Unit was that he wanted to talk to Gavin Sutherland. The sergeant had indicated that they might have been able to capture images from the security cameras at the airport. That would be a big help if those pictures were clear enough. Of course, it would also build a fresh fire under Vivienne. She'd be so ready to hit the streets and begin canvassing businesses around the station and the promenade, it would take him, her boss and half her fellow K-9 officers to hold her back.

What had bothered him most was the way he'd felt sharing the safe house. It hadn't been nearly as difficult an adjustment as he'd originally assumed. He cooked, she cleaned up after

him and the dog provided comic relief. How long this arrangement might have to last troubled him. Wanting to capture her stalker took precedence, yet he knew he would miss their closeness when it ended. He'd almost made the mistake of saying so that morning, but saved himself by switching to saying he'd miss the dog.

Caleb wheeled into an open parking spot along the street that fronted the station. Some kind of a ruckus was occurring directly in front of the entrance.

"I tell you, Rory's my dog," a man shouted.

Caleb circled and joined Vivienne and Hank at the curb. "Do you know who that guy is?"

"Yes." She pulled a face. "His name is Joel Carey. He's been here before, claiming that a stray German shepherd and her puppies we're housing in the kennels belong to him. Belle and Emmett Gage rescued the mama dog from where she was hiding under a porch and brought her here, thinking she'd been abandoned."

"I take it he has no proof of ownership."

"None. No papers, no microchip, nothing. They found her here in Brooklyn so we call her Brooke."

"That guy sounds crooked to me." Giving

the argumentative man a wide berth, he led the way inside.

"We thought so, too. That's why we still have possession of the dog and her pups. The plan is to train Brooke as a working dog and hopefully her pups, too. We all adore them."

"Isn't it kind of chancy to bring in a stray? What if she's sick?"

"Our vet examined Brooke and her puppies. And besides, they were kept isolated until we were sure they were healthy," Vivienne assured him. "Caring for our working canines always come first."

Wondering how soon he should mention the video enlargements, Caleb was headed for Sergeant Sutherland's office when Penelope, her brother, Bradley, and a PD officer hailed them. "Over here."

Because Vivienne went, Caleb did, too. She was in her element here, while he felt like an outsider. Being an FBI agent didn't give him special status in the elite K-9 unit. It was comprised of the best of the best and he respected every member. Especially one of them.

Penelope was hugging Vivienne. Bradley was patting her on the back. The detective with the name tag reading "Walker" was grinning as if he knew her well. They were offering moral support for all she'd been through with

the kidnapping and attempts on her life. The conversation then turned to another case. As Caleb listened, he learned that the men were part of a contingent that had been scouring Coney Island for a gang of smugglers that apparently had it in for one of the K-9s.

Vivienne spoke aside to include Caleb. "Officer Noelle Orton's K-9, Liberty, broke up an arms-smuggling ring and cost the criminals a lot of money, so they've put a high bounty on Liberty's life." She huffed. "See? I'm not the only member of this unit with enemies."

He nodded, sorry that the brave K-9 and her trainer were under siege. "Yes, but the dogs aren't trained to shoot back," Caleb said soberly."

# NINETEEN

The moment Vivienne laid eyes on the printout from the surveillance video, she knew these were the right women. If she hadn't promised to stay in the building while Caleb interviewed Lucy, she'd have taken the telltale images and hit the streets then and there. As it was, Willow was slightly late bringing the sweet three-year-old to her appointment and that wait seemed interminable.

When Willow and Nate arrived, Lucy took one look at the assembled adults and hid behind Willow Slater.

"It's okay, baby," Willow said gently. "When we're done here I'll take you over to play with the puppies. How's that?"

The little blonde girl nodded.

Vivienne felt Hank pull on his leash. He was normally very well-behaved so that drew special attention. Clearly, the sympathetic border

collie was concerned for the feelings of the child.

"Can I pet him?" Lucy asked. "I like him."

"Sure," Vivienne said. She let him approach. Lucy had been to the station many times and was familiar with all the K-9s.

The gentle dog pushed his nose against Lucy's hand. Vivienne didn't stop him because she could see a slight change in the child's demeanor. "It's okay to pet him as long as I say you can," Vivienne offered. "He can tell you're a little bit unhappy and he wants to make it all better."

None of the adults interfered. Vivienne wasn't supposed to be part of the interview, but she did seem to be helping. Silence reigned as the three-year-old shyly put out a hand. Hank's lick of her fingers made her giggle. That set off the K-9 and his tail wagged his whole rear half.

"He's happy to see you again. See?"

"Uh-huh."

Vivienne could have cheered to hear Lucy speaking. "Hank likes it when I sit with him." She patted the floor off to the side. "Would you like to join us?"

Without answering verbally, the child plopped down next to Vivienne and was greeted with a swift doggie kiss that made her laugh more.

She threw her arms around Hank's ruff, burying her face in the silky fur.

"Can I give him a cookie?" Lucy asked.

"Maybe later. Do you like cookies?"

"Uh-huh. Chocolate chip is my favorite."

"I love chocolate chip, too." At this point, Vivienne looked to Caleb and received a thumbs-up, which she took as an okay to further help prep Lucy for the interview. She smiled at her K-9, who had rolled onto his back, tongue lolling, and was silently begging for a tummy rub. "Here," Vivienne said, demonstrating, "scratch him where the white is. See? He loves that."

Little curled fingers sent loose fur flying. Vivienne laughed softly. "Maybe not quite so hard, okay?"

"Okay."

Planning to set the stage for questions about the stuffed monkey toy that was left at the scene of Lucy's parents' murder, Vivienne brought up a different kind. "I hear you like dolls and teddy bears and stuffed toys like that red fuzzy one that giggles when you tickle him."

"Uh-huh." Her smile was wistful. Leaning over the prostrate border collie and hugging his fur, she said, "I miss Andy."

"Andy?" Vivienne saw Caleb and Nate leaning forward to listen.

Willow approached and squatted down next to the child. "Who's Andy, honey?"

"You know."

Caleb joined them. "No, Lucy, we don't. Tell us about Andy. Where did you meet him? In the park, maybe?"

That was way too much attention for the shy little girl. She pressed her lips together, shook her head vigorously and once again buried her face deep in Hank's silky fur.

Vivienne sent a sour look at the FBI agent, clearly expressing a negative opinion of his pushiness.

Not deterred, Caleb asked, "Do you mean Randy, Lucy?"

By that question, Vivienne understood that Caleb was asking if Lucy meant Randall Gage. She held her breath.

"No!" Lucy started to get teary-eyed. "Andy."

Caleb stood and backed off to speak more privately with Gavin and some of the others. "That's not exactly what I intended to ask but it's enough to confirm my original conclusions. I don't think the two sets of killings are related other than a possible copycat situation. My profiles indicate that Randall Gage is re-

sponsible for only the McGregor parents, not the Emerys. Time will tell if I'm right."

Leaving Lucy hugging Hank with Willow sitting close by, Vivienne got to her feet, too. She walked over to where the group was standing, away from Lucy's delicate ears since details needed to be discussed. "So we have neglectful parents in both cases and the possibility that somebody in their lives thought it would help the children to make them orphans?"

"I suspect that contributed," Caleb said. "The killers definitely had a soft spot for little kids. In the McGregor case it's probably a good thing Bradley was at a sleepover and wasn't home that night. He's a lot older than his sister and might have been considered adult enough to be held responsible, too."

"Praise the Lord," Penelope said.

Until now, Bradley McGregor had remained silent. He slipped a supportive arm around his sister. "For us, being taken in by the lead detective on our case and his wife was a lot better than staying at home had been. Our adoptive parents are both gone now but we'll never forget what they did for us. Penny was too young to realize how neglected we were, but I remember sneaking food from my friends' houses and bringing it home to her." He gave his sister an

affectionate squeeze and she leaned her head on his shoulder.

Bradley's words got Caleb thinking. "I'd like to see the Emery neighbors interviewed again. We'll be looking for anybody who showed interest in Lucy or sounds critical of her parents."

"I wish I could help more," Willow said as she bent to lift Lucy into her arms.

Lucy immediately hugged Willow's neck and hid her face from the other adults, the same way she had when she'd been on the floor with Hank.

"Willow, when was the last time you saw your brother?" Caleb asked.

"Like I told the investigating detectives on scene that night," Willow said, "it was when I brought the family food. I'd insisted he either cleaned up his act or I'd be forced to call Child Protective Services for my niece's sake instead of enabling him the way I had been."

"Would you have called?" Vivienne asked.

"I never had to decide." Unshed tears glimmered in Willow's eyes. "The last time I stopped by he'd seemed better. When I couldn't reach him by phone a week or so later, I got concerned and swung by his place." She sniffled. "That's when I found them."

Vivienne was sympathetic. "I'm so sorry."

"I'm going to Sergeant Sutherland's office to submit my official profile," Caleb said. "Briefly, I see the perp as being male, in his twenties, involved in other crimes, probably including drugs, and quick to pass judgment. He's likely to be local which is why I want the neighbors canvassed again—and asked about an Andy. One or more of them may also have been friendly with Lucy, so pay special attention to first names or nicknames that sound like Andy, too."

"I'm going with you," Vivienne said, signaling Hank to come to her side. "The sooner I can get Gavin's permission to hit the streets looking for the women in the printout, the sooner I'll be able to get back to living a normal life."

Whether anyone else noticed or not, she saw Caleb flinch. He didn't need to tell her he didn't want her out on the streets. It was evident. She also knew that her boss might side with him, so she began to mentally prepare a rebuttal in the event she was ordered to stand down. That was not going to happen. Not as long as she had one more breath of life in her.

The notion that she might be in mortal danger wasn't new. She'd faced that fact when she'd pinned on her badge. The notable dif-

ference now was that she didn't like the idea of not being around Caleb Black anymore.

The portent of *that* thought was anything but welcome.

Caleb figured he knew exactly what was about to happen in Gavin's office. His senses were on high alert. His pulse was beginning to speed up. Like it or not, he was in for a fight, one he felt he had to win.

He presented his printed report, then said, "I've sent you the file electronically, too. If there are any changes in the future I'll notify you by email."

"Fine." Gavin peered past him at Vivienne. "Was there something else?"

"Yes," Caleb said quickly. "I'd appreciate it if you'd keep your gung-ho officer off the streets while we search for the women who are stalking her."

"Do you feel Armstrong is a poor risk? Has she done anything to indicate she's unstable or unsuited to patrol?"

"No, but..."

Gavin smiled at Vivienne. "Then I see no reason to refuse to let her search. If anybody has a stake in this, it's her."

Vivienne stepped forward. "Thank you, Sergeant."

Caleb wasn't through. "Her dog could use backup, too, if Vivienne's out there. Surely you have to agree since Hank's not trained for protection or attack." Gavin looked at Vivienne. At her nod, he turned back to Caleb. "I'll send along others who are," Gavin told him. "I know Belle and Justice are free. And Noelle can take Liberty out as long as she's not working a high-profile case. They can defend Hank or Vivienne if necessary."

"I didn't say I needed that much help," Caleb insisted.

"The more coverage, the better," Gavin said. "You don't all have to stay together. Just keep your radios on and let me know if there's any sign of either of the blonde women in the photo."

"Yes, sir." Caleb didn't try to hide his negative feelings, but agreed because it was his only option. That, or wash his hands of the whole case and head back to Manhattan now that his original assignment was complete. The idea of doing that turned his stomach and he figured it was best to leave the office before Gavin changed his mind about letting him join the search.

Vivienne beat him to the door and left it open as she exited.

"Vest!" he called after her.

"Yeah, yeah. I'll get mine from my locker and meet you and the others in the alley between here and the training building. That way the dogs will have access to grass and we won't have to keep stopping."

Only a handler who thought of the K-9 first would have planned that, Caleb told himself. Vivienne and the others were special. No doubt about that. And he was relieved to have extra K-9s on the hunt with them. It was just as well since most, if not all, of his concentration would be focused on the woman he had come to admire so highly.

Part of him supposed he should say something about it to her while he had the chance. A more sensible part disagreed. One reason for limiting siblings or married couples from working together on the streets or in patrol cars was the tendency to be easily distracted. Nothing could ruin a person's awareness of threats like the presence of a loved one.

That conclusion set him on his heels. Loved one? He didn't have anybody like that in his life anymore. Or did he?

His vest fit snuggly beneath his suit coat and shoulder holster. He pulled on the jacket, wishing the weather was cooler, and headed for the meeting place.

It was unacceptable to think he might have

become too fond of Vivienne in the brief time they'd been together. Ridiculous. He was already spoken for. He had a wife. He…

An attempt to bring Maggie's face into focus in his mind failed miserably. Caleb gritted his teeth. He couldn't allow himself to forget her. She'd been too important, too well loved.

Yet what about now? Was it even possible to love twice? As deeply as he had loved once before? He'd believed that impossible until very recently.

Long, purposeful strides carried him out into the alley where the search party was assembling. There were other officers and K-9s there already, but he saw only Vivienne.

When she smiled at him, he knew the truth.

"God help me," he muttered under his breath. "I'm in love with Vivienne Armstrong."

He strode boldly into the center of the grassy strip and raised his hands to claim everyone's attention. "All right. You have your assignments and printouts of the women we're looking for. Video has shown that they frequent this neighborhood and the Brooklyn Heights Promenade, so concentrate your efforts in those areas. Treat the suspects as armed and dangerous whether you see a gun or not. Any questions?"

There weren't any, so he nodded. "Let's go."

Vivienne's presence when she joined him was palpable. The worst thing he could do was reveal his feelings when they were about to search for criminals, so he kept silent. He did, however, meet her gaze, and for an instant he was certain he saw the same emotion reflected there.

Wishful thinking? he wondered. If it was all in his imagination he had to accept that. And if, once he did speak his heart to her, she chose to reject him, he'd have to accept that, too.

Caleb steeled himself against that possibility and headed out onto the street. Right now, they had a job to do and his was to keep the second great love of his life alive.

Failure was not an option.

# TWENTY

Vivienne managed to keep her nervousness hidden from the humans, but Hank was aware. That couldn't be helped. She and her K-9 were supposed to be in tune with each other so it wasn't his fault he was behaving oddly.

Unfortunately, Caleb did notice. "What's the matter with your dog?"

"He's okay."

"He is not. I've learned to read him since we've been stuck at the safe house and he's definitely not okay. So what's the deal?"

Vivienne sighed and confessed. "He's picking up vibes from me and they're making him uneasy. That's why his head is down and his tail is tucked."

"Why are you uptight? Do you expect to spot the women we're after or are you just jumpy because Gavin chose to add so many big protection dogs to our party?"

"Hank may not be crazy about that, either,

come to think of it," she said, wishing she hadn't already admitted to being ill at ease. "We're usually alone or with other trackers when we're working."

"Well, at least the kid you tracked and rescued before is out of danger. I can see why that's made your enemies mad."

"Yeah." She huffed a chuckle. "Mad enough to shoot at me a few times and then try to run me down at the airport. At least they didn't shoot at me or ram us when we were playing tag on the highway. I don't want them to endanger innocent civilians."

"We will catch them," Caleb said flatly. "Even if they change their hair and clothing, we have that ankle tattoo to look for."

"Right. The orange lotus flower. It's a good thing it's still summer. We'd never spot it in the winter when everybody is wearing boots instead of sandals."

"Another good reason to nab them soon," Caleb said.

She could tell he was scanning faces in the crowd the same way she was. "I'm glad you reminded me of the tattoo. I was forgetting to check feet."

"You do feet and I'll do heads," he said. "We're less likely to miss them if we divide the job."

"I suspect Hank may alert, too," Vivienne offered. "I'll keep one eye on him while I look down." If her dog hadn't veered left at that moment she would have walked into a lamppost. "Oops."

Caleb grabbed her arm, pulled her sideways and steadied her. "Tell you what. You look down and I'll keep you out of trouble."

"I assure you I'm able to walk without assistance."

"Tell that to the post you almost hit. And the cement one at the airport."

"I had help there," she joked back, grinning, before freeing her arm.

His reluctance to let go caused her to glance at him again. The depth of his blue gaze reminded her of the summer sky where it met the ocean and its intensity took her aback. "Caleb?"

"Just watch where you're going," he said gruffly as he dropped his hands to his sides.

She considered asking him for his thoughts, then decided against it. Just because she was smitten with him didn't mean it was wise to share feelings, particularly now.

Sun alternated with shadow as they passed beneath store awnings and between buildings. Caleb had already donned his reflective sunglasses, but she'd left hers behind so she had

to rely on the bit of shade provided by the bill of her official baseball cap. The logo in the front identified her as a K-9 officer, as did the patches on her uniform shirt and the lettering on Hank's halter. Because of that, pedestrians tended to give her and Caleb a wider berth than normal.

"See anything yet?" he asked.

"Nope. I can't get a good look at the sides of anybody's ankles. I wish she'd gotten a garland of flowers that went all the way around."

"Picky, picky, picky."

"Yeah, well, you can hardly blame me."

A crackling message came in over her radio. Vivienne cupped the ear containing the receiver and stopped, touching Caleb to get him to halt with her.

"What is it? Did one of the others spot them?"

Vivienne hushed him with the hand holding Hank's leash and listened carefully. Finally, she looked up. "Belle thought she spotted one of the women, but it was an innocent blonde on her way to lunch with a friend."

"There are going to be more sightings like that around noon," he commented. "I never realized how many blondes there were in New York until we started looking for specific ones."

"Yes. Too bad hair coloring is so popular.

Genetics like the ones that produced your hair aren't that common."

"Genetics? You mean like what gives Hank his white feet and chest and tail tip?"

"Speaking broadly, yes. It's most confusing when you have one breed of dog that comes in assorted colors, like Labrador retrievers. They're…" The closing of Caleb's hand around her wrist and his tight grip stopped her in mid-sentence. "What is it? What do you see?"

"Up there. Ahead on the right about half a block. I know that's a long way away but something about one of those women getting out of a cab caught my attention."

"She's looking this way!" Vivienne pivoted to face him so she wouldn't be noticed staring. "Now, look past me. Is she still paying attention to us?"

"I think so." His lips pressed into a thin line and he cupped her shoulders. "Let's step aside and switch positions so you can get a better look."

Vivienne could hardly wait for a second peek. "It's possible. We're too far away to tell. How are we ever going to get closer without scaring her off?"

"Cross the street." He glanced at the last corner they had passed. "The light's green. Come on."

She nearly tripped over Hank's leash as they sprinted for the crosswalk.

Caleb suddenly drew her into a doorway. "Stand back. She's crossing over."

"Which way is she going?"

"Up that next side street," he said. "Come on. If we hurry we can move parallel and overtake her."

"Wait. Running all that way may not help. Suppose she goes into one of those stores before we arrive? Or maybe she has a car waiting for her. We'll lose her."

"What do you want to do?"

"Circle the block with Hank while you trail her that way." Vivienne pointed. "Belle is only two blocks over and coming this direction fast so Hank and I will have backup if I need it before I meet up with you again."

"No way."

Vivienne was so frustrated she was angry. "Okay. Stand here wasting time while my stalker gets away if that's what you want. There's an alley halfway up the block. I'll cut through there and try to get ahead of her. If you were behind her…"

She evaded Caleb's hands as he made a grab for her and took off at a fast jog, Hank falling in at her side and keeping pace. She didn't have to

look back to know that Caleb had not followed. The sense of his presence wasn't with her.

All she could hope at this point was that he had heeded her sensible instructions and would be in place to provide backup by the time she ambushed the suspect. This was it. She could feel it. They'd be one giant step closer to catching a kidnapper and stalker within the next few minutes.

Breathing hard, Vivienne nevertheless managed a smile and a wordless prayer of thanks.

Caleb was dumbfounded when she took off like a world-class runner leaving the starting blocks.

Some battles were worth fighting. This one was not. He spun on his heel and started for the corner where they'd seen the blonde woman get out of the taxi.

Despite the rapid walking habits typical of many New Yorkers, he had to dodge and weave between pedestrians in order to have any hope of reaching the corner before Vivienne emerged from the alley. Sergeant Sutherland hadn't issued him a radio and since it wasn't a part of his normal gear he hadn't considered a need until now. He and Vivienne were expected to stay together and use hers. *Yeah, right.*

Perspiration dotted his forehead and trick-

led down his temples. Between the oppressive heat and the bulletproof vest he was wearing, he was baking alive. But he pressed on. How much longer would it be before Vivienne confronted the blonde woman and ascertained whether she was their quarry?

Sure, it had occurred to him they might be wrong. That was possible. Anything was, unfortunately. As much as Caleb wanted to capture the criminal duo and remove the ongoing threat, he hoped they were pursuing the wrong person this time because Vivienne was temporarily on her own. He needed to be there, to be with her, to protect her if it became necessary.

Skidding around the corner, he touched the sidewalk briefly with one hand, pushed himself back up and regained speed. Shops passed in a blur.

He peered into the distance. "Where are you?" Not only did he not see Vivienne, but he also didn't see any blonde women the right height and age, either.

His cell phone vibrated in his pocket. Slowing to a fast walk, he answered. "Black."

"I lost her," Vivienne said. "Where are you? Do you see her?"

"No. Never mind where I am. Where are you?"

"I stepped back into the alley out of sight

when she wasn't visible on the street. We'll need to check each store she passed."

"Maybe she got by you. Stay there and wait for me. I'll look in stores as I pass but we don't have time to do a thorough search. Not if she's ahead. It'll take too long."

"You're right. I'll have Belle Montera and her K-9, Justice, check businesses as they work their way toward us."

Caleb wanted to cheer. "Once in a while I actually am right," he said.

"Well, don't take too much time to celebrate. I'm not quitting."

"I never imagined you would." He was already on the move again, this time walking rapidly. "I don't have a radio. Did you notify the other K-9 pairs of our possible sighting?"

"Yes. Open channel on the radio. 'Bye."

"Wait. Stay on the phone with me." He waited for affirmation. "Vivienne?"

She was already gone. He thumbed redial. The call went to voice mail. The short hair on the back of his neck prickled. His heart was already racing from his run. Now, it sped even more.

Caleb rose on tiptoe to look for her. If she'd left the alley by now he'd be able to spot her with Hank. But, no. A nearby light standard provided a slight elevation at its base. By lean-

ing out and bracing one shoe against it, he was able to gain another eight or ten inches.

There! There she was. Someone—a woman with long, dark hair—had stopped her mid-block and engaged her in conversation. That scenario was all wrong. It didn't fit Vivienne's insistence on continuing the search or mesh with what she'd told him moments before.

He saw her glance his way, so he waved his free arm, hoping, praying she'd spot him. It was impossible to tell if she had.

Caleb jumped down and hit the sidewalk running. At least he knew where she was and that she was still okay. All he had to do was reach her and everything would be fine.

Closer. Closer. Dodging, pushing people aside when he had to, he tried to act polite when he wanted to shout at them all to get out of his way.

A clearer view was short-lived. Caleb gasped. Vivienne had left Hank sitting obediently on the sidewalk and was approaching the street where a black car idled. The rear door was open.

"Vivienne!" he yelled. "Stop!"

Passersby closed in. Blocked his view. Stole the sight of her and left him so bereft he stumbled. "Vivienne!"

# TWENTY-ONE

Vivienne had seen the frantic-looking, dark-haired woman leave an idling car in the right-hand traffic lane and jump out. She wore dark glasses but her panic was still evident.

"You're a cop," the woman had said. "You have to help me! My son…"

Immediate concern had taken precedence and Vivienne halted. "What's wrong, ma'am?"

"He's—he's choking. I was driving him to the hospital but he's turning blue." The woman's long, thin fingers tightened around Vivienne's arm. "Please! I don't know how to do CPR."

Forgetting everything else, Vivienne had headed toward the car with the mother. At the curb she'd put Hank on a sit-stay and dropped his leash.

"Have you checked the boy's airway?" Vivienne asked.

"No."

Reaching for the mic to her radio, Vivienne wasn't too surprised when the woman tried to stop her by making a grab for it. "Calm down, ma'am. I'm going to request an ambulance. It'll only take a second."

"My son!" It was a wail. "He's dying and you're wasting time talking."

"All right." She continued to request medical assistance as she moved toward the car. "Is he in the back seat?"

"Yes. On the floor."

"What?"

She bent to look inside, seeing a pile of blankets that she assumed covered the child. Of all the ridiculous things to do. In this high August temperature the poor kid was probably having a heat stroke instead of choking.

"Don't crowd me," Vivienne ordered. "Please." She'd placed her left hand on the seat and was reaching for the blankets with her other while the woman pressed in behind and bumped her. "You need to give us breathing room."

Then she felt pain in her head and a hard push, lost her balance and tumbled headfirst into the car. Half on the seat, half on the floor, she reached for her gun by instinct.

The holster was empty!

Vivienne tried to turn, to regain her balance,

but she was too dizzy. Someone slammed the car door into her ankles, making her double up and pull her feet inside. The door banged shut. She reached for her phone—that was gone, too.

She heard Hank barking viciously outside the vehicle and managed to thank God that she hadn't brought him closer.

Horns were honking. The car lurched into traffic. Vivienne's stomach roiled and she tasted blood from biting her tongue.

The woman who had tricked her was sitting in the front passenger seat while someone else drove. Both people were laughing. "See how easy that was?" one of them said. "I told you it would be. She's so softhearted she had to come help my *son*."

"What're we gonna do with her, Mama?"

"Shut up. I don't know. But you can be sure it's not gonna be pretty." She whipped off her long brown wig and tossed it aside, revealing the blond hair everyone had been looking for.

"It won't help you find that little boy again, you know."

"I told you. His name is Tommy. He's my baby brother. I was supposed to be watching him and he wandered off. I've been looking for him all my life. I could hardly believe my eyes when I spotted him right here in Brooklyn."

Listening, Vivienne could tell that one of

her abductors was mentally unbalanced and was also in charge. The mother ran the operation, as Caleb had predicted, so things were definitely not in her favor. Still, when it came to plotting assault or even murder, maybe she could convince the daughter to defy her vindictive parent. If the younger woman refused to listen to reason, she didn't know what else she could do.

The holdout gun strapped to her ankle fit her hand perfectly as she slid it free of its holster. Rising slowly, she kept waiting for her vision to clear and her head to stop spinning. Whatever her captors had hit her with had obviously done some damage. She could only hope it wasn't long-lasting because she needed to get control of this situation ASAP.

Blinking rapidly and praying she'd be able to function efficiently, Vivienne pushed herself into a sitting position, extended her arm and pressed the muzzle of the gun to the back of the older woman's head, then ordered, "Stop this car."

The passenger merely cackled. The car's driver screamed, "Mama!"

"She ain't gonna shoot me in the back," the older woman said, still clearly amused.

"I said, pull over," Vivienne insisted.

"Should I?" the driver asked.

"What do you think? Listen to how scared she sounds." The mother was grinning as she turned to face Vivienne and said, "Drop your gun."

Vivienne was not about to comply. She gritted her teeth against the pain in her head and the throbbing in her ankles where the woman had slammed them in the car door. "Not a chance."

"Then I'll have to shoot you," the old woman said, producing a black automatic weapon and swinging it to bear on the back seat.

"You'll be dead as fast as I am," Vivienne said bravely. "I can't miss at this distance." Although her insides were trembling, she managed to keep her voice steady.

"No, you probably would kill me if you shot," her nemesis said. "Tell you what. Instead of me shooting you, suppose I kill this other gal? Does that change your mind?"

Vivienne was stymied. She might choose to risk her own life to end this standoff, but she would not risk the life of a civilian. For all she knew, the younger woman was innocent of wrongdoing, just as she was. There was only one proven criminal in the car and she was now aiming at her own daughter. What kind of person even considers doing that? she wondered.

"All right. Lower your weapon and I'll lower mine," Vivienne said, waiting for the woman in the front seat to make the first move. She had no intention of relinquishing her gun.

Instead, her older captor reached over and jerked the wheel. The car swerved wildly. A wave of dizziness washed over Vivienne and by the time she'd regained her balance the woman had closed her hand over the top of Vivienne's smaller pistol and twisted it out of her hand.

The speed of the car and the danger to innocent bystanders would have kept the K-9 officer from pulling the trigger even if she hadn't been so dizzy, as the captor had undoubtedly assumed.

Everything was over in seconds. Vivienne sat back, temporarily defeated by her spinning head and her strong moral code.

In the front seat, the older woman was chuckling while her younger look-alike wept as if she was barely able to see to drive.

"Stop sniveling and find a place to pull over. We need to tie up this cop so she behaves herself."

If ever there was a right time to pray for deliverance, this was it, Vivienne thought, but all she could come up with was a heartfelt "Father, help."

If she could have gone back in time and made a different decision she would have listened to Caleb and stayed with him. Now that it was too late, she wished mightily for the chance to tell him he was right. In person. And hopefully not with her final breath.

Caleb used his phone to notify the K-9 unit's headquarters and was patched through to Gavin in his patrol car.

"That's right," Caleb nearly shouted. "I saw them take her. Black sedan. New York plates." He recited the letters and numbers he'd seen.

"I'm close to your location. Which way were they headed?"

"Up 65th toward the Gowanus Expressway, unless they turn."

"Okay. Stay put. I'm almost there."

The rise and fall of one cycle of his siren was all Gavin used when he swung to the curb. Caleb was waiting with Hank. The dog jumped into the car first, then bounded over the center console into the back seat as if he'd done it a hundred times.

Caleb pointed. "That way!"

"Code three?"

"No. I wouldn't use lights and sirens. If they think they've gotten away they'll be less likely to speed or drive evasively."

"Good point. Officer Armstrong did manage to request an ambulance before you saw her shoved into the car. Are you sure it's them? I thought the vehicle we were looking for was tan."

"It's them. It has to be. Either they had two cars or stole one that Vivienne wouldn't recognize."

Gavin immediately radioed Dispatch, giving his other officers the car's full description. "And tell Eden Chang I want a trace on that license. Agent Black thinks it's probably recently stolen so have her start there."

Hearing "affirmative" didn't calm Caleb's nerves one bit. "I told Vivienne to stay with me but she was determined to do this her way. We'd almost joined forces again when she was shoved into that car."

"Why would she allow herself to be drawn that close?" Gavin asked.

"Good question." Caleb continued to scan the thick traffic ahead, hoping against hope to spot the right car. "I have to assume she thought there was a strong need to deviate from her original task." He felt Hank's hot breath on his neck. "I can't understand why she left the K-9 behind, though."

"Because she didn't feel he was going to be a help in her current situation?"

"Possibly. Probably. I'm glad she did. If they leave the car he'll be able to track her."

"Only if we find it," Gavin reminded him. He pushed a button on his dash and the red traffic light ahead of them switched to green, allowing them to pass.

Caleb nodded. The chances of finding the right car in a busy place like Brooklyn were slim and none. Yet they had to try. *He* had to try. And keep trying no matter what. It seemed impossible that they would simply stumble on Vivienne as they randomly drove. The futility of that option settled over him like a lead weight and blotted out the sunny day as if a dark cloud covered the city.

In retrospect he wished he'd given in to the urge to follow her instead of taking orders. That had been a tactical as well as an emotional error. He'd wanted so badly to increase their opportunities to capture her stalker that he'd temporarily lost sight of the possibility that danger could come from another source. That, and she'd upset him when she'd insisted on getting her way.

"It's my fault," Caleb said. "I should have stuck closer."

"That was a judgment call," the sergeant said. "Any of us might have done the same thing. Don't second-guess yourself."

"I thought…" Caleb stopped before expressing his negative opinion of something he already knew was important to Gavin Sutherland.

"What? What did you think? Anything might help us. You know that. So talk."

"It's not a clue," Caleb admitted ruefully. "It's personal."

"Such as?"

The guy wasn't going to quit, was he? Well, it wouldn't make any difference if he aired his grievances. "I told Vivienne I'd given up on praying, and on God, but when all this started with her, the safe house and all, I started to pray again."

"And?"

"And, look what good it did me. Vivienne's been kidnapped, we don't know the names of the women who took her or where they were going. Does that sound like answered prayer to you?"

"Hmm." Continuing to weave in and out of traffic and change lights to green as needed, Gavin finally spoke. "Were you a committed believer once?"

"Yes. I'd dedicated my life to Christ."

"And something, probably your losses, turned you away?"

"I was mad at everybody and everything, even God."

"That's understandable. Do you think God gave up on you just because you gave up on Him?"

Caleb frowned at him. "I'd never thought of it quite that way."

"Well, do. And be ready for answers to your prayers. You may not like what those answers are, but they will come. Eventually."

"Soon would be nice."

Gavin chuckled. "Yeah. Soon would be very nice."

The radio had been providing brief bulletins as they drove. Gavin handed the mic to Caleb. "Keep them posted. I'm going to stay on 65th until we see something or another unit spots them."

"Copy." Being careful not to grasp the mic so tightly that he keyed it and broadcast before he was ready, Caleb peered out to get his bearings.

"Sutherland and Black passing Sixth on 65th," he told Dispatch.

"Brooklyn K-9 copies." There was a brief pause. "Be advised, a black car matching the description of your kidnappers' has been spotted stopping under the Gowanus Expressway at Fifth."

"Almost on scene," Caleb replied. He leaned forward as far as his seat belt would allow and stared into the shadows beneath the elevated highway overpass.

His racing, pounding heart made him momentarily light-headed. "There!" He pointed with his whole arm. "Over there! That's the car."

As she was lying on the rear seat, Vivienne had slipped one hand up and tried to open the door. It was locked. That wasn't a big surprise, but it was disappointing because it limited her escape options. If they decided to get on the expressway they'd be traveling so fast she wouldn't dare jump out even if she could get the door open later.

From the front seat she'd heard a harsh "Over there. Park over there," and had realized her only chance might be coming.

The driver had sniffled. "Right on the shoulder? In front of everybody?"

"We're not staying. I want to get into the back seat with our guest and have a little chat while you take us out into the country, like we planned."

"Mama, really… I think you should let her go. I mean, she was just doing her job."

"Ha! If the cops had done their jobs when

Tommy disappeared I wouldn't have had to keep searching for him all these years. My mama and daddy are gonna be so surprised when I finally bring him home."

At this point, Vivienne was fairly sure she understood the delusion that drove the older woman. She was reliving her childhood and the traumatic loss of her little brother, thinking she had seen him again and that he'd been taken from her by the police.

*By me*, Vivienne added. *She blames me for something that probably happened before I was born.*

The engine noise echoed louder. Movement ceased. Vivienne peeked out and saw that they had stopped beneath a cement overpass. She only had a rough idea where they were and had lost her earbud when she was shoved into the car so she'd been unable to listen to radio chatter. She figured if she could key her mic, even though she wouldn't hear responses, it might help the department track her.

That meant moving and possibly tipping off her captors. Given the fact that one of them was getting into the back seat with her, she decided to hold off.

The moment she saw the round, dark hole at the end of the gun barrel that was pointing

at her again she wished she'd loosened the mic when she'd first thought of it.

"I'm sorry about Tommy. About your little brother," Vivienne said when the older woman shoved aside her legs and forced her to move over.

Her aim never wavered. "Get back here with those zip ties and fasten her wrists together. Now!"

Another door clicked open. Vivienne felt hot air. Smelled gasoline fumes. No cars stopped, so clearly the women were being surreptitious and not looking like they needed assistance.

Gesturing with the gun, the mother ordered her to turn and present her hands to the daughter. As she complied, Vivienne mouthed, *Please?* It brought a corresponding look of chagrin but no change in the circumstances.

"Sorry," the younger woman said, sniffling more. "Mama knows best."

"You know she's sick, right?" Vivienne was whispering.

"She's my mother. I love her."

"Then help her by doing the right thing. She needs to see a doctor."

"I'm sorry," the woman said, tightening the plastic tie so it held fast.

Vivienne's heart dropped along with her spirits. This was not looking good. Now that

she was partially immobilized, her situation was even worse than before.

Several ideas occurred simultaneously. All involved getting herself out of the car before it moved again. The armed woman was less likely to fire at her own daughter despite the earlier threat, so getting a hold on her was probably the best choice. Plus, the daughter was markedly less antagonistic so she'd probably give way more easily.

But that gun. It was a smaller caliber than Vivienne's duty weapon but still potentially lethal, particularly at such close range. Therefore, that had to be her first target.

She prayed wordlessly for support and discernment. The younger woman was turning to get back out. Her mother also retreated slightly. It was now or never.

Vivienne swung her right foot toward the gun. She gave a mighty lunge, kicked the revolver loose while ducking, then pushed off against the floorboard and hurled her body out the opposite door, taking the younger woman with her.

They landed in a heap as a gun went off under the overpass, sounding louder than usual because of the echo.

Vivienne rolled off her younger captor and

scrambled to her feet, still battling recurring waves of dizziness.

On the opposite side of the car her assailant had apparently dropped the gun when it had fired and was down on her hands and knees, searching for it beneath the sedan.

Knowing that running would make her a perfect target, Vivienne dragged the adult daughter to her feet and looped her bound wrists over the woman's head like a noose. It wasn't perfect but it couldn't hurt. Hopefully, her assailant wouldn't realize that a bullet, fired at close range, could pass through one person and also wound the second.

*Just the way it did with Caleb's former family*, Vivienne added. Was this shooter mentally unbalanced enough to shoot her own daughter in order to get revenge on a police officer?

Maybe. She didn't want to find out.

# TWENTY-TWO

Caleb bailed out of the patrol car before it came to a complete halt, drew his gun and raced toward the scene of mayhem. So did Hank.

Barking and growling, the usually placid K-9 was a blur as he made a beeline for the crouching older woman, hit her like a football linebacker and knocked her over. Then he stood, growling, with his bared teeth right next to her cheek, as if daring her to move.

Knowing Gavin was right behind him, Caleb left one kidnapper to the dog and the sergeant while he went straight for Vivienne. To say he was glad to see her was the biggest understatement of his life.

"It's okay, honey. I've got you," he said as he holstered his gun, lifted her joined wrists over her prisoner's head, then got out his pocket knife to cut the zip tie.

Tears were streaking Vivienne's cheeks.

"She tricked me. She said her little boy was choking and when I went to help…"

"I saw her push you into the car but I was too far away to stop her."

"My fault," Vivienne said. "All my fault. I should have listened to you." The moment her hands were unbound she wrapped both arms around him and held tight.

That was more than fine with Caleb since Gavin's requested backup had arrived from the opposite direction and those officers were taking charge of the prisoners and evidence while Gavin led Hank away to the safety of his patrol car.

Caleb began to rub Vivienne's back as he held her. There was no way he could even begin to express the love he was feeling. It encompassed him, went so deep into his heart he thought it might burst. This woman, this stubborn, determined, wonderfully dedicated woman, had to become his wife. She just had to. The only thing holding him back was the fear that she wasn't ready to hear all that yet.

Shuddering signaled the end of her weeping. Caleb laid his cheek against her hair and waited. He started to silently pray—*Please, God*—then realized he should offer thanks instead. Thanks that she had survived. Thanks that he and Gavin had arrived in time. Thanks

that the kidnappers had decided to pull over and were seen. Thanks for each detail that had led to this extraordinary moment.

When he whispered, "Thank You, Jesus," Vivienne raised her glistening brown eyes to meet his. He'd never seen a lovelier, more amazing sight.

"You're back," she whispered. It wasn't a question, it was a celebration.

Caleb nodded. "Yes. And I'm never abandoning my faith again. It's a miserable way to live."

She smiled slightly and whisked away remaining tears. "I wish I were a part of that vow," she said.

"You were. You are. Meeting you helped bring me back."

Lowering her lashes, she spoke quietly, just for him, as the noisy world rushed by all around them. "I don't mean believing in God, I mean the part about never leaving."

His hands cupped her cheeks and lifted her face to his. Was she saying what he thought she was saying? If he let this moment pass he feared he might never get another chance when she'd be this open to his confession, so he sighed and began to speak. "I don't intend to disappear from your life. Ever. And I want you in mine for as long as the Lord gives us."

When her trembling lips parted, he shushed her with a tender kiss. "Hear me out. I know this is way too soon to be admitting I love you, but I don't want anything to interfere with what we have together. Someday, I'd like to ask you to marry me. I know you said you wanted a lot of kids and I thought I'd never be ready for a family again, but everything has changed. Everything."

She was blinking away fresh tears. "How can you be sure?"

"I don't know. Don't have a clue. Some of the alterations in my mindset were so slight I almost missed them. I know we'll need to sit down and talk all this out before you're certain about a future with me but I'm willing to wait as long as it takes."

"That long, huh?"

Caleb studied her expression. Could she be teasing him? At a time like this, when she'd almost died and he'd poured out his heart to her, was she making a joke?

He released her and started to step back. "You think I'm kidding."

Her soft hand reached out and caressed his cheek. "No, no. It just struck me funny that I've been hiding how much I loved you so it wouldn't scare you away, and now I see we we've both been acting nonchalant for nothing."

"You love me? You're sure?"

Vivienne nodded. "Yes. I love you just as you are…or were. Without reservations. Until a few minutes ago I thought you'd go back to your job and forget all about me once this case was solved. That made me so sad I could hardly think straight."

"Never," Caleb vowed, embracing her again.

A grin lit her face despite her damp cheeks. "I get that now. That's why I was teasing you. It's made me so happy I'm giddy. Acting silly. Feeling so much joy I could dance." She sobered slightly. "If I wasn't so sore from being pushed around I might do it."

Caleb looped one arm over her shoulders and started to guide her toward a waiting ambulance. "Come on, then. Let's get you checked out."

"Not yet."

"Haven't you learned that I don't take orders well?"

"Haven't you learned that I'm going to keep giving them?" She chuckled. "I didn't mean I wouldn't let the medics look over my injuries. I meant, I want at least one real, genuine, Caleb Black kiss first."

"Here and now? In front of your boss?"

"Oh, yes. The best you've got, Mr. FBI

Agent. Go ahead. Sarge is busy and not even looking our way."

"Well," he drawled, grinning. "If you're sure."

"I am so sure it's mean to make me wait." She pointed to her lips. "Lay one on me."

"That's not the most romantic invitation I've ever gotten," he said. Then he leaned closer and tried to give her more than she had asked for.

When she opened her eyes again and looked at him he had to laugh. "Good enough?"

"Uh-huh. Whew!"

Caleb was equally impressed. As he lifted her in his arms and carried her to the ambulance, he mentally thanked God for answers to his prayers. They weren't exactly made to his order, were they? That thought was oddly comforting because the results were far better than anything he'd imagined.

Life was going to be different going forward because he was different. In a good way. He worked his old wedding ring off his finger and slipped it into his pocket. After seven lonely years he was going to have a family again.

# EPILOGUE

Vivienné had been more than ready to admit her feelings for Caleb. What she hadn't thought through was how they could make a marriage work when they were both in law enforcement and both knew the daily risks and dangers. Would he be able to accept that she was a cop and a dedicated member of the K-9 unit without panicking every time he knew she was working?

Conversely, she thought she'd be okay with his future FBI assignments, but what if they sent him out of New York? What then? Would she go crazy with worry?

By the following day, when he was helping her move back into her Brooklyn apartment, her fertile imagination had come up with dozens of obstacles to their mutual happiness. She knew her nervousness was evident, she just didn't know how best to bring up the subject.

Caleb solved the problem for her when he asked, "Are you sorry already?"

"What? No!" She slipped her arms around his waist. "Are you?"

"If I was, I'd say so. I expect the same honesty out of you."

Standing her ground, she prayed he'd understand what she was trying to say without getting upset. "I think too much. I keep coming up with reasons why we can't be happy together and it's killing me."

"I know what you mean."

"You do?" Her spirits began to lift.

"Sure. How do you think I went from being a miserable widower to being ready for a new life as a husband and maybe even a father? As I fell in love with you, I kept thinking up reasons why we couldn't be happy or why I wasn't the right man to make you happy."

"Happiness is an inside job, not a feeling dependent upon circumstances," Vivienne said. "You can't make me *be* anything, any more than I can do things that guarantee you're always going to be delighted with me. That would be a terrible burden to have to bear."

"I'm not sure I understand."

"When you accepted a terrible event as something that could not be changed, you were able to anticipate a better future. Nobody could

force you to let go, it had to come from inside you. You chose joy over grieving."

Laying her cheek on his chest, she listened to the steady beat of his beloved heart as she went on. "Joy can bring happiness, sure, but it's so much deeper. I believe it comes from knowing God cares and from trusting Him. We all fall short at times. That's human nature. But beneath all the sorrow and angst and beyond all the terrible things we have to deal with on the job, there is a divine peace that's beyond explanation. I think you'll be able to accept that I'm a cop now."

Caleb pulled her closer. "I can, Vivienne. You did a great job of explaining."

"Did I? Well, don't expect deep spiritual discussions from me on a regular basis. It's taken me a long time to get this far and I know there's a lot more I have yet to figure out."

She felt laughter rumbling in his chest as he said, "I have no doubt you will tell me all about it. So when are we getting married?"

"Are you proposing, Agent Black?"

"You could say that."

"Well, okay, as long as Hank approves," Vivienne said sweetly.

Hearing his name, the border collie jumped to his feet and began to spin in circles, clearly

anticipating something exciting, like a long walk.

Vivienne laughed and clapped her hands. "Good boy! Shall we all go to the *park*?"

Since Caleb had dressed more casually on his day off she didn't hesitate to take his hand and pull him toward the door. "Come on, handsome, our furry family member wants to go out." She slowed and sobered slightly so he would know she was taking his marriage proposal seriously. "We can go to the promenade and people watch while we plan our future. We'll need a home with a yard like the FBI safe house, for starters. We'll support each other in our jobs. We were both meant to be out there helping people."

His nod and wide grin warmed her heart. "Is that all?"

So filled with joy and anticipation she could hardly stay quiet, she chuckled and gave him a look that she hoped conveyed even a tiny bit of her elation. "Oh, no," she drawled. "I'm just getting started."

When Caleb made a face and said, "That's what I was afraid of," she erupted into laughter that echoed down the corridor of the apartment building.

"Will you settle down and get serious for a second," he asked.

"Why?"

The moment he pulled her back into his arms and gave her another kiss, she had her answer. No words were necessary.

* * * * *

*Look for Jackson Davison's story,*
Scene of the Crime, *by Sharon Dunn,*
*the next book in the True Blue K-9 Unit:*
*Brooklyn series,*
*available in September 2020.*

*TRUE BLUE K-9 UNIT: BROOKLYN*
*These police officers fight for justice with*
*the help of their brave canine partners.*

Cold Case Pursuit *by Dana Mentink,*
*October 2020*

Delayed Justice *by Shirlee McCoy,*
*November 2020*

True Blue K-9 Unit Christmas: Brooklyn
*by Laura Scott and Maggie K. Black,*
*December 2020*

Dear Reader,

*Trust is the key to unwavering faith. Faith is the key to trusting God.* When I wrote that I was probably as surprised as Caleb and Vivienne. And blessed to have been able to express something that has often bothered me. The same goes for losing a spouse. There is no way to go back, no way to continue as you were, either. Nothing is the same, nor will it ever be.

Once Caleb—and I—came to that conclusion we were able to see new possibilities for happiness. There is no forgetting, there is only change and finally acceptance. No two people grieve exactly the same way. God reaches out to us and offers comfort. It's up to us to accept it.

If you feel lingering sadness, I urge you to turn to the only one who will never disappoint if we let Him help us. Jesus is never far away.

You can contact me by email, Val@Valerie-hansen.com, or catch me on Facebook. Oh, and remember this is a work of fiction. Most couples do not find real love this quickly!

Blessings,
*Valerie Hansen*

*Valerie Hansen*

# Get 4 FREE REWARDS!

## We'll send you 2 FREE Books plus 2 FREE Mystery Gifts.

**Love Inspired** books feature uplifting stories where faith helps guide you through life's challenges and discover the promise of a new beginning.

FREE Value Over **$20**

---

**YES!** Please send me 2 FREE Love Inspired Romance novels and my 2 FREE mystery gifts (gifts are worth about $10 retail). After receiving them, if I don't wish to receive any more books, I can return the shipping statement marked "cancel." If I don't cancel, I will receive 6 brand-new novels every month and be billed just $5.24 each for the regular-print edition or $5.99 each for the larger-print edition in the U.S., or $5.74 each for the regular-print edition or $6.24 each for the larger-print edition in Canada. That's a savings of at least 13% off the cover price. It's quite a bargain! Shipping and handling is just 50¢ per book in the U.S. and $1.25 per book in Canada.* I understand that accepting the 2 free books and gifts places me under no obligation to buy anything. I can always return a shipment and cancel at any time. The free books and gifts are mine to keep no matter what I decide.

Choose one: ☐ **Love Inspired Romance Regular-Print** (105/305 IDN GNWC)  ☐ **Love Inspired Romance Larger-Print** (122/322 IDN GNWC)

Name (please print)

Address                                                                           Apt. #

City                                    State/Province                          Zip/Postal Code

**Email:** Please check this box ☐ if you would like to receive newsletters and promotional emails from Harlequin Enterprises ULC and its affiliates. You can unsubscribe anytime.

### Mail to the **Reader Service:**
**IN U.S.A.:** P.O. Box 1341, Buffalo, NY 14240-8531
**IN CANADA:** P.O. Box 603, Fort Erie, Ontario L2A 5X3

Want to try 2 free books from another series? Call 1-800-873-8635 or visit www.ReaderService.com.

*Terms and prices subject to change without notice. Prices do not include sales taxes, which will be charged (if applicable) based on your state or country of residence. Canadian residents will be charged applicable taxes. Offer not valid in Quebec. This offer is limited to one order per household. Books received may not be as shown. Not valid for current subscribers to Love Inspired Romance books. All orders subject to approval. Credit or debit balances in a customer's account(s) may be offset by any other outstanding balance owed by or to the customer. Please allow 4 to 6 weeks for delivery. Offer available while quantities last.

**Your Privacy**—Your information is being collected by Harlequin Enterprises ULC, operating as Reader Service. For a complete summary of the information we collect, how we use this information and to whom it is disclosed, please visit our privacy notice located at corporate.harlequin.com/privacy-notice. From time to time we may also exchange your personal information with reputable third parties. If you wish to opt out of this sharing of your personal information, please visit readerservice.com/consumerchoice or call 1-800-873-8635. **Notice to California Residents**—Under California law, you have specific rights to control and access your data. For more information on these rights and how to exercise them, visit corporate.harlequin.com/california-privacy.        LI20R2

# Get 4 FREE REWARDS!

## We'll send you 2 FREE Books plus 2 FREE Mystery Gifts.

**Harlequin Heartwarming Larger-Print** books will connect you to uplifting stories where the bonds of friendship, family and community unite.

**FREE** Value Over **$20**

# THE WESTERN HEARTS COLLECTION!

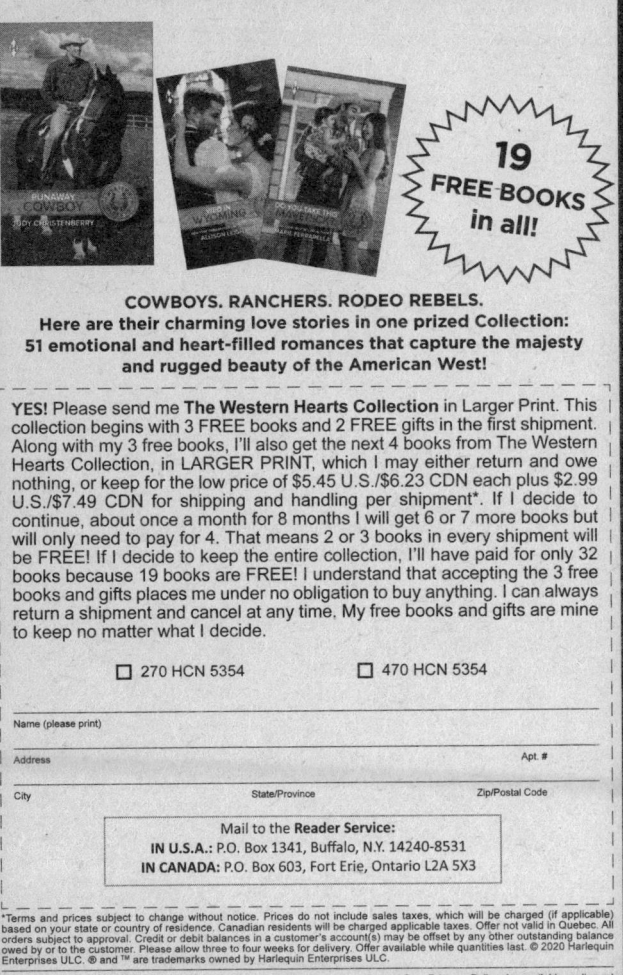

**19 FREE BOOKS in all!**

**COWBOYS. RANCHERS. RODEO REBELS.**
Here are their charming love stories in one prized Collection:
51 emotional and heart-filled romances that capture the majesty
and rugged beauty of the American West!

**YES!** Please send me **The Western Hearts Collection** in Larger Print. This collection begins with 3 FREE books and 2 FREE gifts in the first shipment. Along with my 3 free books, I'll also get the next 4 books from The Western Hearts Collection, in LARGER PRINT, which I may either return and owe nothing, or keep for the low price of $5.45 U.S./$6.23 CDN each plus $2.99 U.S./$7.49 CDN for shipping and handling per shipment*. If I decide to continue, about once a month for 8 months I will get 6 or 7 more books but will only need to pay for 4. That means 2 or 3 books in every shipment will be FREE! If I decide to keep the entire collection, I'll have paid for only 32 books because 19 books are FREE! I understand that accepting the 3 free books and gifts places me under no obligation to buy anything. I can always return a shipment and cancel at any time. My free books and gifts are mine to keep no matter what I decide.

☐ 270 HCN 5354        ☐ 470 HCN 5354

Name (please print)

Address                                                           Apt. #

City                          State/Province               Zip/Postal Code

Mail to the **Reader Service:**
**IN U.S.A.:** P.O. Box 1341, Buffalo, N.Y. 14240-8531
**IN CANADA:** P.O. Box 603, Fort Erie, Ontario L2A 5X3